Praise for
Jill McGown
and
A PERFECT MATCH

"A smoothly professional first novel with elements of low-key police procedural and traditional puzzle . . . And the answers lend to a tidy solution at the close of a neat, unpretentious, pleasantly readable debut."

The Kirkus Reviews

"In the classic tradition of challenging whodunits, A PERFECT MATCH is a complex mystery where all the clues to the puzzle are out in the open—yet even the most canny sleuth will find it difficult to deduce the solution."

Mystery News

Also by Jill McGown:

RECORD OF SIN
AN EVIL HOUR
THE STALKING HORSE
MURDER AT THE OLD VICARAGE*
GONE TO HER DEATH*
MURDER MOVIE*

*Published by Fawcett Books

A PERFECT MATCH

Jill McGown

FAWCETT CREST • NEW YORK

A Fawcett Crest Book
Published by Ballantine Books

Copyright © 1983 by Jill McGown

ISBN 0-449-21810-4

This edition published by arrangement with St. Martin's Press, Inc.

Printed in Canada

First Ballantine Books Edition: December 1990
Fourth Printing: April 1993

CHAPTER ONE

THE SEPTEMBER DAWN CREPT OVER THE SKY LIKE water on blotting paper, spreading a fine, thin light to supplement the yellow glow of the street lighting. In the town centre shopping precinct, photo-cells registered the increase, and the anti-theft store lights clicked softly now and then, obediently switching themselves off. The street lamps, made of sterner stuff, remained on duty—except one, and even that obstinately glowed a dull, dying red. The clock set into Marks and Spencer's wall displayed 6:11 in liquid crystal, and the town slept on, unaware of the coming of the new day, unaware of the milk on the door-steps, unaware that the rain which had lulled it to sleep had moved on, following the thunder northwards.

The town centre was built on the edge of a hill, a hill once part of the forest which still existed in patches of now more manageable woodland round the new town. Here and there it was allowed to invade the town itself, bringing a little wildness to the unnatural order of a town which had been decided upon, like so many others, in the early fifties. The trees in the heavily wooded parkland at the foot of the hill swayed slightly as the light breeze stirred their branches, and the birds sang, thankful for the storm that had washed away the dust of the long summer. Some had left the trees for the line of semis which stood beside the wood, and the luxury

1

of a bath in the rainwater gathered on the flat roofs of the garages.

The road was busy during the week, busy enough for mini-roundabouts to have broken out like measles all along its length wherever there was a junction; but on a Sunday morning, even when the grey light had become established, the road was empty and quiet. The hum of an engine broke the stillness, and a police car came down the hill from the station, along the line of semis, towards the wood itself, following the curve of the road to the far end, and pulling across to a lay-by. A young policeman, too tall for the compactness of the Panda car, walked on to the soft, heavy ground, crazed and bare in patches, and crossed diagonally to the footpath.

The boatshed-cum-café lay hidden by the trees, and beyond it the artificial lake, spreading back into the wood, the way the car had come. The policeman followed the footpath past the building, across the small parking area, round the water's edge. The ducks swam eagerly towards him as he squelched past, but he had no scraps of food, no time for the ducks. Disappointed, they turned and swam in their own wake, bobbing reluctantly under the surface now and then to make him feel bad.

The creatures who knew the wood at night scattered as he came, darting for safety into the thick undergrowth, making it shiver, releasing drops of rainwater. They knew she was there; they'd known all night.

And now, as he involuntarily closed his eyes, so did the policeman.

Helen Mitchell waved her hand through the steam that rose from the black, traditionally sobering coffee.

"It won't do much good," Donald said, casting a glance at the sofa. "It's a bit over-rated, if you want my opinion."

Donald's opinion wasn't something that Helen wanted too often these days; their twenty-six years of marriage had seen to that. But she was glad he was there, all the same. Chris sat hunched on the sofa, his eyes technically open, his brain almost working.

It had been just before six when Helen had been wakened by the doorbell ringing continuously, like a fire alarm, and gone downstairs to see Donald opening the door to a drunk and dishevelled Chris, shirt-sleeved and shivering.

She'd seen him like that before, his dark hair bedraggled, his chin stubbled with the beard that grew so disreputably fast. At first, Chris Wade had just been a name to Helen; a friend of Donald's, someone he had done some work for, someone who gave him the occasional round of golf. But two years ago, all that had changed, and Chris had become a responsibility.

Now, despite all the water which had flowed under the bridge since, they seemed to be back where they started. Helen helped him hold the mug, when it had cooled enough not to be dangerous, and he drank some of the coffee. His eyes moved with difficulty towards her. He looked even younger like this, and she felt like the mother-substitute she had once been.

"Where's Julia?" she asked him again, for the umpteenth time. "Is she at your house? Chris?" She shook him gently, but he didn't have to answer. Both she and Donald had rung the number repeatedly in the past hour, and there had been no reply.

"I didn't mean to," Chris said. "I didn't mean to." It was all he had said, virtually. Over and over again.

"Didn't mean to what?" Donald tried. "What didn't you mean to do?"

"She made me," he said. "We went to the café."

Each time, the conversation had gone the same way. Each time, Helen had looked across at Donald, who was clearly worried; despite the fleshiness with which middle-age disguised his features, he looked almost haggard. Each time, he'd just looked away.

"Is she here?" Chris asked suddenly, trying to struggle up from the sofa, spilling coffee as he did so.

No, she wasn't there. Julia was Donald's sister-in-law, and their weekend guest; Donald had snapped that he wasn't her keeper when it had become apparent that she was spending

3

the night elsewhere. His brother Charles had died only a few weeks ago, but Julia had not allowed her loss to affect her too greatly. It had surprised Helen a little that she wasn't even playing the part of the grieving young widow; she wanted his affairs settled quickly, to get the money for which she had married him, and run. If that had been all there was to it, then only her lack of courtesy should have concerned Donald and Helen when she went off with Chris and failed to return. But of course, that wasn't all there was to it.

It concerned Helen, in a way that she had no intention of explaining to Donald, who thought that extra-marital attachments were his prerogative. It was certainly true to say that Julia's nocturnal activities held no interest for her, as she had indeed said; what she had omitted to say was that Chris Wade's did. And she was certain that it concerned Donald more than he admitted, certain that his relationship with his sister-in-law had ceased to be platonic long before Charles succumbed to his third heart attack. He had been making unfunny jokes in the clipped, off-hand way that he did when he was upset, because Julia had gone off with Chris and had not come back. And Helen had felt like laughing, in spite of it all, at the symmetry of the betrayal.

But now, she had no desire to laugh. Julia wasn't with Chris. Chris was here, saying that he hadn't meant to do it, he hadn't meant to do it.

"Do what?" she asked again, in an urgent whisper, as Donald shrugged and left the room.

Alone with Chris, she squeezed his hand in encouragement. "It'll be all right," she said.

"I didn't mean to. I'm sorry," he said. "She took me there—I didn't mean . . . I shouldn't just have left her there."

Donald's normally smooth brow was creased with worry as he sat looking out of the spare bedroom window, through the gloom towards the wood, and the boating lake. Chris had been there—he'd said so, more or less. Why? Why would she take him there? His fingertips massaged his brow, then tapped it rhythmically. What had happened? Why had he come here? He'd got drunk, and then come here. Why? Donald dropped his hand to continue its drumming on the windowsill. As he tried to make some sense of the monosyllabic utterances from Chris, the frown grew deeper, furrowing the skin between his brows. Donald's smoothness of countenance was not the result of a blameless life, free from worry and regret; his was the smoothness of the beach-pebble, that has been buffeted by the wind, moved and turned by the sea, kicked by children, scraped by sand, wearing smoother and smoother, and harder and harder.

Long-sighted, these days, if anything, he focussed on the sweep of road that separated the old wood from the newer pine wood. At the far end sat a car, its rear lights just visible in the increasing daylight, and it was this to which Donald gave his attention as the questions went through his mind. Another car drew up beside it, its unnecessary headlights lending it an air of urgency. There could be no mistaking the activity at the other end of the road, when the two cars were joined by police squad cars with their flashy orange stripes. As he watched, a police mini-bus passed the house and drove along to the knot of cars at the lay-by. Uniformed policemen got out, one after the other, like one of those joke films, disappearing into the trees that sheltered the boating lake.

"What are you looking at?"

He jumped slightly at the sound of Helen's voice, but he couldn't find his own to answer.

"He's sobering up," she said. "He hasn't said what happened yet—he said he wanted time to think."

Donald moved to one side in an invitation to join him at the window. Her eyes met his.

"Oh God," she said. "God help him."

It was a prayer, not a profanity. Donald moved away from the window, and stood helplessly aside.

"A car's coming this way," Helen said, her voice flat. "Two cars." She switched on the bedside light.

Donald rubbed his eyes, hoping he'd wake up, and none of this would be happening. Chris couldn't have killed her.

5

She couldn't be dead. But all those police—he sat on the edge of the bed.

"They're stopping here," Helen said, coming away from the window. "He's done something, Donald." Her grey eyes were tinged with green as she looked at him, as they were when she was tired, or excited, or crying; she had cried too often, he told himself with uncharacteristic honesty. She automatically checked her appearance in the mirror, smoothing down her sleep-tousled hair, still blonde, though here and there streaked with grey. She pulled her housecoat more neatly about her comfortable proportions.

"He's done something," she said again, to his reflection, as the doorbell rang.

They went downstairs, and Donald opened the door to the police.

"Detective Inspector Lloyd," the senior man said, nodding to the constable, who walked back to the car. The other car was just parked, with two policemen in it. Donald still couldn't find his voice.

"Stansfield CID," he continued, with just a trace of a Welsh accent. He had the uncomfortable look of a bearer of bad tidings. "I believe you may know a young woman—Julia Mitchell? Is she a relative?"

Donald nodded miserably. A time like this, and all he could think was that Inspector Lloyd was small for a policeman.

The coffee had unscrambled part of Chris's brain, allowing him to move more or less as he intended, but his eyes were still reluctant to work properly. There was someone at the door. Wasn't it very early? Maybe not, but it felt early. Too early for visitors. Holding a steadying hand out towards the bookcase, Chris made his way to the door. From the hallway, the voices were muffled and urgent; he shook his head and frowned with the effort of concentration as he gently eased up the lightswitch until it clicked quietly, and the curtained room was dark. Opening the door a crack, he could hear, if not entirely follow, the conversation.

6

". . . afraid I have bad news, Mr. Mitchell."

"Where is she? What's happened?" Helen's normally deep voice, higher pitched than usual.

"She had your address in her handbag, you see—"

"What's happened, Inspector?" Helen, impatient.

The inspector lowered his voice, and Chris couldn't hear what was being said, but the reactions were unmistakable. He took a deep breath, and tried to clear his head. She was dead. *Dead.* But that didn't make any sense.

". . . sorry to have to bring such bad news." The Inspector cleared his throat. "Do you know a Christopher Wade, sir?"

"Wade? Yes—I know someone called Wade—"

Donald was playing for time. Giving him a chance. Chris looked round the room, lit by the strand of light from the hallway. What did Donald expect him to do?

"We've reason to believe that Mrs. Mitchell was with him at the boating lake, Mr. Mitchell. You wouldn't know where he is now, would you?"

Chris held his breath. They'd have to tell him. But he couldn't remember, couldn't get it sorted out in his mind.

"No," Helen's voice said firmly, and loudly. "I'm sorry, we don't."

The silence which followed her statement seemed to last forever as Chris picked his way across the room to the patio window, sliding it back noiselessly on its newly replaced runners. The draught from the window caught the door, opening it slowly, with the full horror-film squeak that it always gave, flooding the room with light.

"Perhaps I could come in for a moment?" the inspector asked.

Chris slipped out into the garden, and slid the window back. The cold morning air that might have cleared his head just made him feel giddy; he made a dive for cover before the already suspicious inspector started looking for him. Crablike, he ran towards the end of the garden, which backed on to the pine wood, and looked back at the curtained house. His foot caught the top bar of the fence as he jumped, and he crashed to the ground, wrenching his ankle. He dragged himself into the wood, crouching below the cluster of new trees. His breath, sharp and cold, was no longer under his control, and he lay on the ground, his eyes closed, gulping air. When at last he could breathe at his own pace, he had time to think. He couldn't stay here. They'd find him, and he still didn't know what to say. He needed time to remember.

He remembered one thing. One place where he could hide, where they might not think of looking. Slowly, painfully, crouching close to the ground, he hobbled away.

Lloyd followed the Mitchells into the sitting room, and noticed the three mugs that sat on the coffee table.

"Is there another person in the house?" he asked.

"No," Helen Mitchell said quickly. "They're from last night, I'm afraid—I had a visitor." She picked up the mugs and took them away.

"May I sit down for a moment?" Lloyd hovered over an easy chair, until Mitchell held out a hand in assent.

Helen Mitchell came back, apologising for keeping him waiting. Both she and her husband looked pale and shocked; both sat quite literally on the edge of the sofa, staring at him anxiously, as he leant back comfortably.

"I realise you've had a shock," he said, looking from one to the other. "And I'm very sorry, but I do have to ask some questions."

"Of course, yes." Mitchell stood up, his right hand in a fist which he hit gently against his left palm, over and over again. "You know," he said, speeding up the little punches and stopping, his hands suddenly helpless, "it's like a bad dream."

Lloyd nodded sympathetically. "What was your relationship to Mrs. Mitchell?"

"Brother-in-law," Mitchell told him, sitting down again, suddenly. "She was married to my older brother. Charles," he added, then looked up, almost apologetically. "He died a few weeks ago," he said. "Heart."

"I'm sorry," Lloyd said, smoothing down the hair at the

8

back of his neck, feeling the thinning patch, feeling his age, as he always did when he'd got the rotten job. People wanted to be alone with their thoughts, and he was here asking questions. He cleared his throat. "And did Mrs. Mitchell live with you?"

"No," Helen Mitchell answered. "She was just here for the weekend. Donald's looking after his brother's estate." She lit a cigarette. "He's a solicitor," she added, as though in explanation.

"Oh?" Lloyd was surprised. "I thought I knew all the solicitors in Stansfield."

"You'll know my firm," Donald said. "Hutchins and Partners—I don't do criminal law at all. Conveyancing and probate."

"I see." You're getting plenty of practice, Lloyd thought.

"I'm actually just the executor of my brother's estate," Mitchell added. "My being a solicitor hasn't got anything to do with it." The last sentence was accompanied by a quick, impatient glance at his wife.

"And Mr. Wade is a friend of yours?" Lloyd addressed the question to Mitchell.

"Yes. Yes, he is."

"Did your sister-in-law know him well?"

"No." Mitchell shook his head. "They met by accident, really."

Lloyd raised his eyebrows enquiringly.

"My brother had a lot of property in this area," Mitchell said. "Scattered about—you know." He was staring at his hands, clasping and unclasping them. "That's why Julia was here."

"I know it must be difficult," Lloyd said. "There's no hurry—take your time."

"You probably know that he owned Mitchell Engineering," Donald continued. "He sold up some time ago—a good few years ago now—but there are other properties which weren't sold with the main works—they're the ones I mean. A couple of grazing areas, a shop—" he looked up quickly, "and the boating lake."

Lloyd was glad to hear a reference to something relevant, and nodded encouragingly.

"It was decided that the simplest course would be to sell these properties off. Julia had no ties in Stansfield—she didn't want to be responsible for property here."

"Quite," Lloyd said.

"I put them in the hands of an estate agent," Mitchell said. "Chris Wade's brother-in-law, as a matter of fact." He smiled briefly. "I know that sounds a bit like jobs for the boys, but he and his wife—Chris's sister—had just moved here, and he'd gone into partnership with a local man. I thought I might as well put some business his way."

Lloyd didn't know or care about the ethics involved, but he supposed Mitchell would get to the point eventually, and listened politely.

"So last night, I took Julia to see him—to discuss various things."

"Could I have his name, Mr. Mitchell?" Lloyd blinked a little as he reached for his notebook. If he'd known he was going to be dragged from bed at six o'clock in the morning, he'd have gone there before two o'clock.

"Martin Short."

"Oh yes. I know him slightly." It was a lie; he didn't know him at all. But sometimes it encouraged them, made them think you were human. You weren't, of course. He certainly wasn't at this time in the morning. He glanced at his watch. It was almost eight o'clock, to his surprise. "Could I have his address?"

Mitchell gave him the address, and stood up. "That's where she met Chris," he said, beginning to pace gently towards the curtained window and back. "He was at the Shorts, visiting his sister."

Lloyd frowned a little. "But she was with you at that point?" he asked.

"Yes—it's a bit complicated." He stopped pacing and stood with his back to Lloyd, then turned. "There was a bit of a problem. About the boating lake." He sat down again, and sighed. "My brother always intended leaving it to the

10

town," he said. "He never got around to putting it in his will, but I knew that he'd meant to. Julia was insisting on selling it to the Council rather than donating it, and I had been trying to make her change her mind."

Helen Mitchell rose at that point as if to leave the room, but stopped, lit another cigarette, and sat down again.

"You pass the boating lake going from here to the Shorts' house," Mitchell said, after the slight diversion. "And Julia said she wanted to check something—I don't know what, now. Probably wanted to count the salt-cellars," he added.

Lloyd permitted himself a small smile.

"I had one last go at persuading her, and it developed into a row. We went on to the Shorts, but we had had this disagreement, and she wouldn't stay. When Chris realised she intended walking back, he offered her a lift."

Lloyd put his pen away. "Well, thank you, Mr. Mitchell. You stayed on at the Shorts, did you?"

Mitchell nodded. "Yes. Not very gentlemanly, but I had had enough of her, to be honest." He sat back, relaxing a little now. "That sounds awful," he said.

"Not at all. Had Mr. Wade met Mrs. Mitchell before?"

"No. That was the first time they'd met."

Lloyd frowned. "So you know of no reason why he'd want to—harm her?"

"Of course not!" Helen Mitchell snapped.

"And you don't know where he is?"

"No," she said.

"You haven't seen him since he left with Mrs. Mitchell?" He addressed the question to Donald Mitchell, who shook his head.

"No," Helen Mitchell said again, in answer to his enquiring look.

He wondered. He wondered about the three mugs that she was so keen to get rid of. Too late now. "One more thing," he said. "Who is Mrs. Mitchell's next of kin? Do you know?"

"It'll be her father," Donald replied abstractedly. "But he's on holiday—Spain, I think."

11

"Then I'm afraid I'll have to ask you to identify her, Mr. Mitchell."

Mitchell closed his eyes. "Yes," he said heavily. "When will you want me?"

"We'll send a car, Mr. Mitchell. Will you be available later this morning?"

"All day." Mitchell rose wearily and pulled open the curtains, admitting the daylight. "Helen? Could you put the light off?"

Helen Mitchell switched off the light, and stood by the door. "Inspector, if you've no objection—I'd rather be dressed if we're to continue talking."

She was no longer in the first flush of youth, but Lloyd could well believe the rumours that Constable Sandwell had assured him were going round about her and Wade. Wade must be ten, perhaps fifteen years younger than her, but there was a kind of youthful bravado there, defying him to get the better of her, that made her look like a girl—like a little girl, defending what was hers. The mixture of vulnerability and defiance was engaging. Lloyd smiled. "I beg your pardon, Mrs. Mitchell. I'll get out of your way now. I'm afraid I'll be back, though."

She didn't move as he walked towards the door. "Do you think Chris Wade killed Julia?" she asked, her voice as calm as if she were asking him if he thought it was going to rain.

"I don't know, Mrs. Mitchell," he said. "I just know I'd like to talk to him, and he's disappeared."

She nodded, and moved aside, to let him leave.

Outside in the car, he sat for a moment, looking up at the settled, comfortable house, before nodding to the constable to drive back down the road to the grim scene-of-crime.

At the lake, the breeze was growing stronger, rippling the surface of the water, making him shiver. Everyone had forgotten how to dress for autumn; one or two of the lads had left their jackets in the bus, from force of habit during the heat wave. He raised a hand to acknowledge their presence as he strode towards the beribboned barriers.

Judy was there now, talking to the doctor, having to raise

her voice slightly above the snapping of the ribbon. She smiled gravely as he joined them, in the way they all learned to do, her brown eyes troubled.

"Morning, Lloyd," the doctor said. "I was just telling your sergeant here—twelve hours at a rough estimate." He pointed a warning finger at him. "But it is rough—don't bank on it. Wait for the P.M."

"We're finished in there," a middle-aged man called from the building.

"Fine—thanks." Lloyd turned to Judy. "Do you want to have a nose around inside? I'll be there in a minute."

He and the doctor watched as she picked her way across the mud to the pathway.

"Detective sergeants have improved a bit over the years, haven't they?" the doctor said, with a grin. "Much better legs than they used to have."

Lloyd laughed. "Don't let her hear you saying that, for God's sake!"

Judy, new to the area, new to the rank, but a long-time colleague of Lloyd's, heard the laughter, and wondered if it was at her expense. She always did, and always had. It was a form of conceit, her mother had told her when she was small. Assuming that people had nothing better to do than talk about her.

The long, thin rectangle of the boathouse had had a small square partitioned off to produce the café, and it was into this section that Judy walked. Windows had been provided as a concession to the customers, but the high trees blocked out most of the light. Judy picked her way through the forest of chairs upturned on the tables, and stood by the counter. The tables and chairs occupied an L-shaped area, and behind the counter, through a curtain of grimy plastic strips, she could see the tiny kitchen that took up the rest of the square.

Her eye travelled over the flaking paintwork on the door, up to the dingy ceiling. The walls were covered in a plastic material of indeterminate hue to about shoulder height, when they became yellowish-white, with hairline cracks running across them like cobwebs. Through the window, still spattered with the night's rain, she could see the hedged courtyard, where hopeful tables presumably used to be placed on promising summer days. There was a desolate feel to the room, now that its surfaces were smudged and dirty where they had been dusted for fingerprints: the counter, the window ledge, the door. The table and chairs that had been used, presumably by the victim and her attacker, were covered with the unhappy smears, and chalk circles marked the bloodstains, small and almost insignificant, the only sign that anything at all had happened.

The floor was tiled with black and white squares, cracking where the uneven floorboards failed to support them. Judy ran her toe idly round the hole that had appeared in the corner of one tile, and sighed. The gloom of the place was invading her, hurting her. She ran her hand through the newly curly hair that Lloyd said made her look like Kevin Keegan, and wished she worked in Woolworth's.

The door opened suddenly, and Lloyd, a little windswept, strode in, shattering the dark silence, forcing the café back into its original mundane role. His Celtic looks gave him a presence that his inches could not command, issuing an unspoken challenge to everything that moved, especially Judy.

"Well?" he asked. "Where the hell were you?"

"You know where I was. Running Michael to the airport. I came as soon as I saw the note."

Lloyd grunted, and joined her at the counter. "So," he said. "How much do you know?"

"Not a lot. I know the girl's name was Julia Mitchell, and that she's the widow of the man who owned Mitchell Engineering originally. Charles Mitchell—was that his name?" She glanced at her notebook. "And we're looking for someone called Wade, who was seen arriving with her and leaving without her." She raised her eyebrows in a question.

"It was reported by a boy—he came in this morning. I'll let you have the details later."

"What's the story, then?"

"She was visiting an estate agent called Short, and Wade

14

was there. He offered her a lift home.'' Lloyd spread his hands.

"Do we know anything about Wade?'' Judy wandered behind the counter to see what she would see.

"Well—she had no reason to be wary of accepting a lift, if that's what you mean. She was staying with her in-laws, and Wade's a friend of theirs—and the estate agent she was visiting is married to Wade's sister, so he did provide references.''

"Her in-laws—is that who you've just been to see?''

"Yes. Donald and Helen Mitchell.''

"What does he do?''

"He's a solicitor. His brother only died a little while ago, and that's why Julia was here—sorting out his estate. I gather she's been dreaming of this ever since she walked down the aisle.''

"She was a lot younger than him, I take it?''

"Must have been thirty years younger,'' Lloyd said. "He died of a heart attack.'' He grinned.

"And Wade's a friend of Donald's,'' Judy said, hoping to chase away the grin and failing.

"So he'd like us to think.'' The statement was accompanied by his Knowing Look, and Judy felt her irritation with life in general settling firmly on Lloyd in particular.

"Oh? And what do you think?'' She brushed through the plastic strips into the kitchen, throwing the question over her shoulder.

"I think he's Helen Mitchell's bit of fluff,'' Lloyd said smugly, following her through.

"Helen Mitchell?'' Judy asked. "Donald's wife?''

"The same.''

"On what evidence?'' Judy opened the oven door and looked inside, for no good reason.

"Oh—just the way she reacted.'' He shook his head. "Not that it gets us much further forward.''

Judy shut the oven door with a bang. "What do you want me to do?'' she asked.

"You go back to the station—there's a file started. Read it

15

through—see if you can follow anything up today. It would be a Sunday, of course. I'll be back as soon as possible, but I'd better see this estate agent person.''

Judy was about to leave, when she saw the door in the back wall of the kitchen. ''The boathouse?'' she asked.

''Yes—it's not locked.''

She pushed it open, and stepped through to find herself in darkness, unable to find the lightswitch. A strip of light showed where the big doors at the end didn't quite fit together, and she could see the shapes of the small boats, as she moved further in. She swore as she banged her hip on the corner of an unsuspected desk. Lloyd followed her in. ''It's smelly,'' she said, sniffing. ''Damp.'' She ran her hand down one of the boats. ''Oh—they're plastic. I thought they'd be wood.''

''Fibreglass,'' Lloyd said. ''They don't need so much maintenance. Which is just as well,'' he added. ''As far as I know they don't get any.''

''Does it actually operate?''

''The boating lake bit does, at weekends. The café's been closed for a while now. It was a grand gesture when Mitchell Engineering was on top of the world and everyone wanted British everything. But they couldn't afford it, really. It doesn't even belong to them now—until last night, it was Julia Mitchell's property, I understand. It'll be a good thing if the Council does take it over.''

Judy felt his hand touch hers, where it rested on the side of one of the boats. In the half-light, she couldn't see his face. The contact could have been accidental or deliberate, in fun or in earnest.

''I'll get back then,'' she said abruptly, pulling her hand away as she turned.

Light flooded the shed, and Judy could see the offending desk just inside the door, where stood the tall, thin form of Constable Sandwell, his hand on the now obvious lightswitch. He tried hard to show no reaction at all to finding them in the dark, while she chose to stare at the grubby phone on the desk. It would have to be Sandwell, she thought. You-Know-What-I-Heard? Sandwell.

"Excuse me," she said, brushing past him. Let Lloyd think of a good reason. Let Lloyd pass it off with a smile. She was getting out of it.

CHAPTER TWO

*"THIS IS NEWSDESK REPORT WITH THE TIME AT
ten A.M.*

*"Reports are coming in that the body of a young woman
has been found in Thorpe Wood near Stansfield town centre.
The body has not yet been formally identified, and police are
not releasing the name at present. It is understood that they
are treating the death as murder, and that a man is being
sought. A full-scale search of the woods is under way."*

Donald listened to these words and these only, and they
remained in his head long after the radio returned to the
inanities of the local D.J. When the music began, he snapped
off the radio and lay back on the bed, waiting for Helen to
finish in the bathroom. He felt tired, but there was no time
to sleep, even if he could, with the horrors of the identification still to come. And more questions—about Chris, and
Julia, and last night. And Helen, of course, had lied to the
Inspector.

The bedroom door opened, and Helen, smelling of warm
terry-towelling and bath-oil, announced that the bathroom
was free. Since the Inspector left, the only topic of conversation had been the bathroom. Outside the house, the Panda
car still sat with its two occupants, and by tacit agreement
not a word was spoken about Julia. Donald presumed that
they were there in case Chris turned up, or perhaps they

thought he was hiding in the house. Donald half-wished that he was.

The bathroom was still steamy from Helen's bath; condensation beaded the windows and tiles. Donald drew a finger through the moisture on the shower panel, his mind on the wood, and the boating lake, and the mean little café. What could she possibly have said or done to make Chris react like that? He switched on the shower, and tried to drench the thoughts. She must have been so frightened. The warm water sprinkled on to his shoulders, trickling down his back, soothing the tension, calming him. He had to be calm, because worrying wouldn't alter anything. No one would know what had happened until Chris was found—conjecture wouldn't help. He didn't know whether he was glad or sorry that Helen had lied to the police. They'd find out, of course—Helen had only recently taken up deception, and it still had an amateur quality.

He rubbed soap over his body in loops and circles of lather. What did it matter if the police did find out she'd lied? What did any of it matter? The whole thing was a mess, anyway. He knew why she'd lied, of course. He had known for a while, though Chris as suitor—Chris as *rival*—was hardly something that would have occurred to him at first. Helen's inability to prevaricate with any degree of confidence had given the game away a few weeks ago, when he had puzzled over something she had said, and in this very room had cut himself shaving when realisation dawned.

Chris, whom he'd rescued like a drowning puppy in a sack, and truthful, loyal Helen were more than just good friends. How much more, he didn't know; it took him all his time to believe that he was right, though he knew he had to be. The incredulity was no reflection on Helen, and no measure of his egoism. It was merely that he knew her, and knew the sleepless nights that her perfidy must have cost. Sometimes, during the three o'clock in the morning soul-searching in which he had occasionally indulged, he had wondered how he would feel if she were unfaithful to him. Every now and then, having left the warmth of someone else's bed to return,

19

with a glib lie, to his own, he'd wondered how he would react if the tables were turned.

When it finally happened, he was slow to realise, then disbelieving, then fatalistic. And quite proud of the discovery that he did not operate a double standard. If he could do it, so could she, because he didn't really care, and he didn't imagine she did either. Their marriage had been grinding along with a flat tyre for years. Every now and then the sparks flew as the metal touched the ground, but they had carried on, at first for the children, and then for convenience. Now, it was bumping and jolting on the metal all the time, and soon they would have to stop and get out.

And anyway, he liked Chris. He didn't want him to be in this terrible trouble, and he didn't understand why he was. Forget it, forget it, he told himself sternly. One thing at a time. Wait and see. No point in meeting trouble halfway. Having exhausted his supply of wise saws, he lifted his face to the thin jets, screwing up his eyes and letting the water cascade over his face. It streamed down his body, washing away the soap and the fatigue and the worry.

What did it matter? The whole thing was a mess.

"I still can't believe it," Elaine Short said, handing Lloyd a cup of unannounced coffee, her hand shaking slightly as she did so. She was tall, slender to the point of thinness, and as elegant and graceful as a dancer. She and her husband were both in their forties—about his own age, Lloyd judged. Martin Short, looking anxiously at his wife, was about as different from her as he could be. He clearly never skipped lunch; he lumbered amiably about the room in search of things he had mislaid—his cigarettes, his lighter, his glasses, the plans of the café and boathouse. His fair hair never stayed where he meant it to, and he flicked it off his forehead as he spoke.

"You read about this sort of thing," he said to Lloyd. "But you never imagine them as real people, do you?" He lit a cigarette, having finally run to earth the necessary equipment to do so. "I mean, you don't think of them as being ordinary."

The Shorts had given him the bare bones of what had happened the night before. What time Donald and Julia arrived, that Julia left very shortly afterwards, that Chris offered to run her back to the Mitchells. They had admitted, reluctantly, that she had refused the offer at first; but then, Elaine assured him, people did, didn't they?

He knew now that Wade was a widower, a piece of information defensively given to him by Elaine, as though it might damage his case.

"Your brother's wife," he asked. "How long ago did she die?"

"Two years ago," Martin answered. "It was a car crash. Chris took it very hard—he was driving." His eyes flicked over to his wife as he spoke. "He blamed himself," he went on. "But it was no one's fault really—a dog ran out. It was just one of those things."

"He's all right now, is he?" Lloyd asked.

"Oh yes. It took him a while—he began to drink a fair bit. Don and Helen were very good to him, I believe." He started looking for an ashtray. "We weren't here then," he added. "We've just moved here." Finding the ashtray, he sank back into the sofa. "That's why it's so hard to believe," he said. "He wasn't drinking or anything." Too late, he realised that the statement presupposed his brother-in-law's guilt. "Not that I think—"

"He didn't kill her!" Elaine Short interrupted him vehemently, bringing down the coffee pot with a thud, and sitting down opposite Lloyd. She didn't share the sofa with her husband as Helen Mitchell had done, and yet Lloyd got a sense of unity from the Shorts that had been singularly lacking from the Mitchells. It was of no importance—he just liked to collect the odd pieces of human behaviour that came his way.

"Nobody knows what happened yet, Mrs. Short." Lloyd sipped his coffee and was pleasantly surprised.

"What happened is that Chris took her home from here, and now she's dead and he's disappeared," she said, succinctly enough. She jumped up, and walked to the window. "And you think he killed her," she added. "Don't you?"

"I don't know, Mrs. Short. Really, I don't. I want to speak to him certainly." He took another sip of coffee. "And," he continued, "it would be silly of me to pretend that he isn't under suspicion, because he is. But I don't know enough yet to have formed any conclusions."

"You don't seem to have to know!" she said angrily.

"Oh?" Lloyd finished his coffee and walked over to her. "What have I done to indicate that?" He stood beside her, looking out at the garden, fresh after the rain, to see yet more rain darken the pathway as he spoke.

"You've got men searching the woods," she said miserably.

"She was naked, Mrs. Short. Her clothes could tell us a lot." The voice was gentle, though the effect of his words was not meant to be.

Elaine Short was staring at him, and then her husband. Lloyd didn't speak, but nodded as she looked back at him.

"Are you suggesting that Chris—?" she didn't, wouldn't, finish the sentence.

"I'm asking for help, Mrs. Short. I want to know as much as you do—as much as everyone who came into contact with Julia Mitchell knows. Then, I can perhaps come to a conclusion. And I don't know until then whether that conclusion will involve your brother or not."

She walked shakily back to her chair, but Lloyd didn't go with her. "So," he said. "You've told me that Donald Mitchell stayed and your brother ran Julia Mitchell home." He stayed by the window, and didn't look round at the Shorts. He could feel the eye-signals, and even see a faint reflection in the window as the clouds raced across, darkening the sky.

He turned, quickly, and they tried to look as though no communication had taken place, like schoolchildren caught cheating in an exam.

"Now," he said. "I'd like to know what they said, what you said, what you thought, even." He sat down then, fixing

Elaine with his eye. "And if you don't believe your brother could have killed her," he said, "you won't help him by missing anything out."

"I don't think Elaine had any intention of—" Martin began, protectively, but he was interrupted.

"No, I hadn't," Elaine said. "But I would, if I thought it would help. There's nothing to leave out," she said simply. "At least, not about Chris."

Martin shifted uncomfortably as his wife looked over at him. "It hasn't really got anything to do with us," he said. "Or what happened, for that matter."

"It might, whatever it is," Lloyd said. "Tell me. If it's got nothing to do with it, no one will ever know I knew." He smiled at Martin with the clear-eyed honest look that almost always worked, and wasn't disappointed.

"They had had a row," Martin said, reluctantly. "Donald and Julia. They were still going at it hammer and tongs when they got here."

Elaine rose, and switched on the table lamp. "She was very angry," she said. "She wouldn't stay."

"Mr. Mitchell did mention an argument," Lloyd said. "I don't think you're breaking a confidence." But there was more, obviously. He smiled at Mrs. Short. "I don't suppose I could beg another cup of that coffee, could I? It just isn't like that when Constable Sandwell makes it."

"Of course." She poured another cup for each of them, and came to a visible decision. "I don't think it really has any bearing on it," she said. "But I—that is, we—we think Donald was having an affair with Julia Mitchell."

Lloyd raised his eyebrows. "I see," he said. "And the row could have been of a more personal nature than I was led to believe?"

"It could have been," she said, as cautiously as he had.

Lloyd stirred his coffee thoughtfully. "What makes you think they were having an affair?"

"Not what they were saying," Martin said. "That could have been about anything. It didn't make much sense unless you'd heard the rest of the row."

23

The coffee was almost gone again. Lloyd tried to make it last, but the cups were very small. "What were they saying?"

Martin screwed up his face as he tried to remember. "He said something about her doing something, or not doing something, and she said that she hadn't promised to."

Setting down his empty cup regretfully, Lloyd asked if either of them could remember the exact words.

"No. I don't think so," Martin said slowly. "They were angry—shouting at each other. I don't know exactly what they said."

"I think I do," Elaine said. "As far as I can remember, he said 'I wouldn't have believed you'd do this,' or something like that."

"That's right," said Martin, suddenly coming to life. "And she said 'More fool you'—I remember that. And then that she'd never promised anything. He said it was a row about the boating lake, but—" he shrugged.

"And what makes you so sure it wasn't?"

There was a silence and Martin's skin became slightly pink.

"Tell him, Martin."

"I don't think it's anyone's business but theirs!"

"Tell him!"

Martin hunched his shoulders like a small boy, then spoke quickly, throwing away the words. "It's nothing really. I had to be in London for a couple of days a few weeks ago, and I stayed the night rather than do the trip twice." He began to search for his cigarettes. "At an hotel."

"They're on the table," Lloyd and Elaine said in unison, then smiled with some warmth at one another.

"I was booking out on the Sunday morning, and I saw Donald and Julia coming down the stairs. It was first thing in the morning."

"Did they see you?"

"No." Martin looked ashamed. "I don't think so. I saw them at the top of the stairs, and I went into the phone box as they came round the corner."

24

"A bit of a coincidence, that," Lloyd said. "Out of all the hotels in London."

"No—not really. It was Donald who suggested I stay there if ever I was in town."

"And he still doesn't know you saw him?"

"No." Martin Short had retreated so far back into the sofa that he was almost invisible.

"Now. Last night. They came in, having a row. How long did Mrs. Mitchell stay?"

"Two minutes," Elaine said. "Not even that."

"They stood there," Martin said, indicating a spot near the door. "I didn't even have time to offer her a drink." He pursed his lips. "Perhaps if she'd stayed—"

"Then he called her a mercenary bitch, and she said she was going," Elaine said. "She'd sooner walk home than stay with him—that sort of stuff. And that's when Chris offered her a lift."

"Right. And when did Mr. Mitchell leave?"

"The storm began just after that, and he waited until after eleven—well after—before he left."

"Thank you." Lloyd rose. "You've been very helpful—and the coffee was delicious." Twelve o'clock, his watch assured him. No wonder he was beginning to feel peckish. "I've been here a long time," he said. "I'm sorry."

"Never mind about that," Martin said. "Just so long as you get to the bottom of it." He was neatly overtaken by Elaine, who followed Lloyd to the door.

"You still think that Chris did it, don't you?" she asked him, as he stepped out into the gusty wind.

He turned back to face her. "I don't have any other theory to consider yet," he said. "You said it yourself—he took her home, she's dead, and he's disappeared. But they're looking for evidence now—it could change the whole picture."

"If you want someone else to suspect," she said, "you try Helen Mitchell. Ask her where she was when Donald tried to ring her—twice. You ask her that—it's her husband Julia was sleeping with, after all!"

* * *

Chris Wade sat in the gloom, his knees drawn up to his chest, his ears straining to hear any sound above the whine of the wind in the trees. There was a window, but years of untroubled grime blocked out most of the watery light. He didn't dare move until it was dark, and he couldn't stand in the confined space. The bench was beginning to assume the comfort rating of a king size double bed, but he must not lie down. He might sleep, and be taken by surprise. He'd made matters worse now, by running away, and the only justification would be if it gave him time. Time to remember, time to make sense of it all, time to go to the police of his own accord.

Helen would be in trouble if they found out he'd been there. He'd tried to tell her; dimly, through the haze of drunken memory, he could remember trying to explain. She had patted him, humoured him, cradled him like a baby. He could feel her arms, soft and welcoming, until he asked her to leave him. And then the police came, and told her Julia was dead. And he, for a single, stricken second, believed he'd killed her. His alcohol-clouded mind told him to run. Donald told him to run, when he took his time answering the police. Helen told him to run, with her direct, atypical lie.

So he had run, and in the safety of his lair, he'd made the mistake of slipping off his shoe to examine his ankle. He couldn't get the shoe on again, which made even giving himself up a difficult obstacle to overcome. But at least his prison was safe—even the vandals had forgotten it existed, and it would be a while before the police remembered. It had seemed so important once—it was an eyesore, a disgrace. But now the tangle of bushes almost hid it, and the good people of Stansfield had forgotten all about it. To Chris it was no eyesore; it was a haven, a safe-house, a resting place where he could have time. Once he'd decided what to say, then he'd go to the police.

It would be nice, though, to lie down. Just for a moment.

* * *

One o'clock, and no more news than they had already given. Helen Mitchell switched off the radio, and poured herself a stiff drink. The gin was possibly negating the less fattening qualities of the slimline tonic, but for the moment she didn't care about her thickening waist. She had never been sylph-like; she was the kind of woman once called handsome. At fifty she was perhaps more attractive than in her youth—age suited her tall, well-built frame rather better than girlishness had. In her teens, she had felt like an Amazon, in her twenties and thirties, unfashionable. During her forties, her robustness had mellowed into a suggestion of overweight, and had made her softer, more approachable. Now she kept an eye on the calories as middle-age spread threatened to make her merely fat.

Donald had gone off with the police to make the identification, and Helen had tried hard to feel something, but she couldn't. She was worried sick about Chris, that was all. Julia and Donald and the rest of the world could, and probably would, go to hell. She wanted to know if Chris was all right.

Last night seemed a long time ago. It had all started when Donald had rung looking for Julia, and had suggested that she and Chris might have gone off somewhere together. The irritation she had felt at the suggestion surprised her. Irritation was the name she had given to the sudden sweep of anger, but jealousy would have been nearer the mark. Chris was her business. She had put down the phone with such force that Margaret, who was visiting, had asked her what was wrong, but she had just laughed it off with "Men!" and there were no more questions, because they had to leave to catch Margaret's train.

At first, she hadn't liked Chris, who had presented himself as a surly, uncommunicative young man, who had usually had too much to drink. She had asked Donald not to bring him to the house, but when he explained about the accident, her sympathy had been roused, and she had taken over the role of keeper, cooking meals for him, listening to him when he was maudlin and berating himself for being the cause of

27

Carrie's death. She had watched the gradual effects of her patient counselling, as he emerged from the self-pity, and his health, both mental and physical, returned. He began to piece together his life and his business, both perilously close to bankruptcy after months of neglect.

Then Charles Mitchell had died, and Donald had to deal with his estate, which meant spending even more time in London, at the Mitchell Development offices. Spending time with Julia. One night, when he rang yet again to say that he was staying over in London, she had told Chris about Julia, and about Donald's other girls. The final, fatal straw had been dropped in place, and the sudden rush of emotion caused their relationship to undergo a sea-change. He was fourteen years her junior, and until a month ago she had been just someone to run to, someone who would put up with him in any mood, in any state. In the last few weeks, everything had changed.

Chris's sister and her husband moved to Stansfield, and perhaps it was Elaine who got Chris when he needed cheering up, because it certainly wasn't Helen. She knew he needed her, and now he was saying he wanted her. She had just begun to believe him, begun to accept that his motive was not one of pity, or gratitude, begun to make less of an attempt at concealment of their changed relationship, when this happened.

The clock had turned back two years when he staggered in, breathing whisky fumes all over her. And Helen knew then that she didn't care what happened to her or anyone else. Chris was all she cared about.

"Mrs. Marsden?" Judy smiled at the lady who sat in reception, even though she had probably given herself indigestion hurrying up her canteen Sunday lunch in order to see her.

Mrs. Marsden was a small woman with a neat figure and greying hair.

"If you'd like to come with me," she said, and Mrs. Marsden stood up.

"I hope it's him you're looking for," she said in a stage

28

whisper. "He wouldn't say." She nodded to Tom Rogers on the desk. "I'll feel such a fool making all this fuss if it's not."

"No need, Mrs. Marsden," Judy assured her, pushing open the swing door into the C.I.D. room. It was quiet now after the controlled excitement prior to lunch, when everyone had gone around trying to look as though it was all in a day's work. Only Joe Miller held the fort.

"They're all out," Joe said, with a sigh. "Or gone back to their own jobs, thank God."

This was a reference to the Superintendent who was, Judy had already noted with relief, back upstairs where he belonged.

"Through here," Judy said, as their heels rang through the empty office. She held open the door to the office she shared with Lloyd, and indicated a chair. "Have a seat," she said. "Bring it up to the desk." She smiled encouragingly. "Now. You think you've got something that will help us?"

"Only if it's him you're looking for."

"Who would that be?"

"Mr. Wade from the garage on Victoria Street."

Judy rearranged some files on her desk. "Is that what you've heard?"

"Everyone says so. You've been at the garage, and it's been closed all day."

"It's Sunday," Judy said.

"It normally opens on Sundays," Mrs. Marsden countered.

Judy smiled. "Do you have some information about him?" She unearthed a piece of paper. "But before we start—can I have your full name and address?"

"Edna Marsden. 27 Livingstone Drive." Mrs. Marsden waited until she'd written the address. "I saw him this morning," she said.

"What?" Judy couldn't remember the last time someone with information really had had information. "When?" she asked.

29

"At about quarter past five."

Judy looked startled. "You saw him at quarter past five in the morning? Where?"

"At his garage—I deliver his milk."

"Oh! I see." Judy laughed, but Mrs. Marsden didn't. "And he was there? At that time in the morning?"

"Yes—he gave me a fright, because I didn't know. You can't see the office light from outside, you see." Mrs. Marsden undid the top button of her coat, getting herself comfortable. She was enjoying herself. She had insisted on seeing Judy as the senior officer—Joe Miller not being good enough. And now she was going to get her money's worth. Still, thought Judy, she really did have information, which was more than she could have expected.

"What happened? Anything?"

"Nothing much—but he was funny. I had just got off the float—I take it right up to the door, you see, and park it behind the pumps. And I was taking the milk out when he spoke, right behind me. He'd got a bottle in his hand, and he was in a state."

"A bottle? He was drinking?" Judy wrote "drinking" on her pad.

"Not that kind of a bottle. A milk bottle."

Judy smiled, crossing the word out again. "But he was in a state, you said?"

"He was. I think he had been drinking—he was upset."

Judy drew a neat dotted line under "drinking," and wrote STET. "Upset?" she queried. "How did he show he was upset?"

"He looked upset. As though he'd just had bad news." Edna stood. "Do you mind if I take my coat off? It's hot in here—I'm sure your heating's up too high."

"Probably. Yes—do take your coat off. How do you mean—as if he'd just had bad news?"

"Oh, you know. He looked pale, and his eyes looked red, as though he'd been crying."

"Where were you at this point?" Judy asked.

Mrs. Marsden stared at her. "At the garage," she said. "That's what I'm telling you."

"Yes, of course. But were you in his office at any time, or on the forecourt—where?"

"Where I said. By the pumps."

"So the only light would be from the street lamps on the pavement?"

"Yes—but I could see all right." That Edna resented the implication, Judy could see by the huffy lift of her chin.

"I know you could," she said quickly. "I'm just thinking about those lights. They make everyone look a little odd, you know. He probably thought you looked pale with red eyes." She laughed a little, but Mrs. Marsden didn't.

"It wasn't just that! His shirt was unbuttoned, and it was quite cold after the thunder. And when he took the milk, his hands were shaking."

"Could you describe what he was wearing?"

Lloyd came in as she spoke, and moved noiselessly to his desk. If Mrs. Marsden only knew that he was an inspector, Judy's days would be numbered.

"Not very well," she said. "The lights make things go funny colours." It was as though she were making a new point, as though Judy had never mentioned the lights' ability to make things look different. "Dark clothes," she said. "That's all. No jacket."

"What sort of shirt was Mr. Wade wearing? Can you remember? Short sleeved, long sleeved? Tie?" She glanced across at Lloyd, who had begun to listen to the conversation. "Was it a dark shirt?"

She thought for a moment. "No—it was light. It could have been red, because his car was there, and it's red. The lights make it go a sort of mustard colour. That's the colour his shirt looked. It had long sleeves—and it was open, so I don't think he had a tie."

"Good. Anything else you noticed about him?"

"Only that his hands were shaking, like I said. Because I said to put the milk down before he dropped it. And he did," she added, with a hint of triumph.

31

"He dropped it?" Lloyd asked, sitting forward.

"He put it down," she replied, with a withering glance in his direction.

Lloyd laughed, but Mrs. Marsden didn't.

At Thorpe Wood, sunlight chased the shadows across the dark surface of the lake as the quickening wind blew the clouds away, and the ducks watched interestedly as the teams of police, who had fanned out from where the body had lain, took a temporary breather. Her clothes had been found, caught up in the tangle of undergrowth. Skirt, blouse and jacket, rolled up together, caught on the thorns of a wild rose-bush. Shoes, some way distant from each other, lying on the ground. No underwear, and no sign of Wade, so they would keep on looking.

The squad cars, Panda cars, private cars, vans and wagons left room for only one lane of traffic. Each car, few and far between, was stopped at the temporary traffic signals, and its passengers questioned. Traffic cones and orange-jacketed police slowed drivers down on every exit road, the men yawning with boredom while they waited for the sparse Sunday traffic. Watchful eyes assessed the handful of people using British Rail's reduced Sunday service; buses were observed, but there was no sign of Wade.

An unmarked car, containing two plainclothes officers, sat quietly in the road that ran down the side of Wade Motors. The building itself had received the attentions of the evidence-gatherers. He wouldn't come back there, but you had to watch, just in case. Another watched his house, another still kept a less obtrusive eye on the Mitchells' house, yet another on the Shorts'. They had just finished in his own house, but they weren't optimistic. There was no reason to believe that he'd been home. Nothing to suggest where he might be now.

By two o'clock, it had settled down to near-routine, but this wasn't routine, certainly not in Stansfield. Drunken stabbings, and domestic rows that got out of hand got headlines in the local papers because they were rare enough.

But this was news, and the ducks were doing well out of

the currently access-denied reporters and film-crews whose estate cars littered the grass. This was murder, not the unintentional result of a frustrated marriage or a night out with the lads. This was Hunt for Killer of Rich Widow. This was Naked Blonde Death Riddle. This would sell newspapers; this would make good television.

This would feed a lot of ducks.

CHAPTER THREE

DONALD THANKED THE YOUNG WOMAN WHO had driven him home, and stepped thankfully from the car into the invigorating breeze. It had been Julia all right. He had had a dread of not being able to tell whether it was her or not, but he could. When it was over, he had felt light-headed, but relief rather than shock had caused the giddiness. He wondered if that was the usual reason for people fainting—your mind building the thing up to such a pitch that you are prepared for anything. And what you feel is relief that it isn't as bad as you thought.

He was a rich man now that Julia was dead. But that wasn't what was in his mind as he looked at her. Some things were more important than money.

Helen shushed him as he came in the door, and he stood to listen to the news.

"The naked body of thirty-five year old Julia Mitchell, widow of the late Charles Mitchell, was found this morning in the woodland round Stansfield boating lake. The police say that Mrs. Mitchell appeared to have been strangled, but that there is no immediate evidence of a sexual assault.

"Her husband, Charles Mitchell, died just seven weeks ago of a heart attack, and Mrs. Mitchell was in the area on business connected with her husband's estate. Her body was found less than a mile from her brother-in-law's house, where she had been staying.

34

"The couple, who lived in London, had strong local connections, Mr. Mitchell being the founder of Mitchell Engineering, the largest single employer in Stansfield. When he retired from the engineering world six years ago, Mr. Mitchell's keen business eye enabled him to make a second fortune in London property development . . ."

The radio went into a rehashed obituary which now included Julia.

"Are you all right?" Helen asked. "You look pale."

"Yes, I'm fine. It wasn't too bad, considering."

Helen held up the whisky decanter. "Drink?" she asked.

"Please."

"Are you hungry yet? I've made a salad, and there's cold chicken."

"Later." He picked up the paper. "Oh—that reminds me. The police want a photograph of Julia—to jog people's memory, they said." He looked at Helen over the top of the newspaper. "It could have been anyone," he said. "It might not have been Chris."

But Helen shook her head. "Have you got one?"

"No, not on me. Why would I have a photograph of Julia?" He turned the page, having read nothing. "That's why I'm telling you. I'll have to go to their place tomorrow and see what I can find. The press are pestering the police for one, anyway. And they want to know where her father's staying in Spain so that he can be told. So I'll have to see if there's a note of that anywhere." He wondered about her definite shake of the head when he suggested someone other than Chris might be "being sought" as the radio put it. "Did Chris say anything to you?" he asked.

"Nothing that made sense." She poured herself a gin and tonic, and Donald noticed the empty bottle of tonic on the sideboard. He hoped she knew what she was doing.

"Helen?" he said, as people only do when they are about to broach a sensitive subject.

She looked across enquiringly, perhaps a little apprehensively. "Yes?" she said, trying to sound off-hand.

"Do you know where Chris is?"

35

She looked faintly surprised. "No, of course not." She looked away. "Why would I know where Chris is?"

The deliberate parody of his reply about Julia's photograph did not serve to make Donald feel any more sanguine. He just hoped Helen wasn't getting herself—and by extension, him—into deep water.

"You could get into real trouble," he warned her. "If you're withholding information—it's an offence." He drank some of his whisky, and waited for it to make him feel just a little bit better, but it didn't.

"You didn't tell them you'd seen him," she said defensively, spearing the lemon slice with the cocktail stick, and freshening the drink with a new one.

Donald knew this mood. The "I'm-going-to-get-tight-so-there" mood that happened once in a blue moon. He wondered how many she'd had.

"Only because you lied to the man!" he said snappishly, then wished he hadn't, because that wasn't the only reason. "And be careful how much you drink, because he'll be back."

"Oh." Helen screwed the top on the tonic bottle. "All right."

Donald closed his eyes. He could see Maria when he was in London. That would make him feel better.

Lloyd looked up. "When you saw him," he said to Mrs. Marsden. "When he spoke and startled you—did you by any chance ask him what he was doing there in the middle of the night?"

"Well, I said 'You're an early bird' or something like that. I don't think of it as the middle of the night," she explained.

"No, quite. Did he say anything?" As witnesses went, Mrs. Marsden was pretty good. And patient—he'd been through the whole thing again with her.

"He said he had a big job on," she said. "But he was slurring his words, and I didn't see how he could be doing anything."

Lloyd nodded.

"And he wasn't wearing old clothes," she volunteered. "Not the kind of clothes you mend cars in."

"It might not have been that sort of job, of course," Lloyd suggested.

"No," she agreed. "But if it was paperwork—you'd probably do that at home. I don't think you'd go to work at five in the morning."

"Possibly not." His stomach was rumbling, and he coughed to mask the sound, sneaking a look at his watch. Two fifteen—why wasn't he at home having roast beef and two veg like other people? For a moment, he wished the divorce had never happened; that when he did go home it would be to his wife and children. But it was only for a moment.

"Well, thank you Mrs. Marsden," he said, standing up and extending his hand. "You have been a considerable help."

Mrs. Marsden submitted limply to a handshake. "People say not to get involved," she said. "But I don't think that's any way to be."

"Quite, quite," Lloyd agreed heartily. "I'm afraid we haven't quite stopped imposing on your time—would you just go with the constable, and he'll write out your statement. It won't take long." All the time, he was ushering her to the door, and now he stood awkwardly, holding it open with one hand and signalling to Sandwell with the other, as Mrs. Marsden wrestled with her coat.

"You'll all catch your deaths," she warned him. "Having the heating on that high in September."

Lloyd smiled uncertainly. The central heating hadn't been on since sun decided to visit Britain for the fourth time in living memory, and it needed an Act of Parliament ever to get it switched on again. When she was gone, he grinned at Judy.

"So," he said. Judy was looking in the drawer for something, and Lloyd took the opportunity of perching on the corner of her desk without being glared at. "What's the story so far?"

She made an exasperated face as she surfaced. "What's wrong with the chairs?" she asked.

"Have you got it all straight yet?" He ignored her complaint.

"A young man—Paul Sklodowski—I've even learned his name, came in on his way to work this morning to say that he was worried about a girl." She glanced at the statement, and began to read aloud.

"I saw the car arrive at the boating lake at about half past eight. There were two people in it, a man and a woman. When it left at approximately nine o'clock, only the man was in it. I took the number of the car in case something had happened." She looked up at Lloyd. "He didn't have anything to do with it?" she asked.

"Not as far as we can tell—he didn't come last night because he thought we'd laugh at him. But he was worried about it all night, and so he came in first thing this morning."

"Do you believe him?"

Lloyd made a face. "I'm not sure. I thought we could go and have a talk with him this afternoon—I haven't seen him myself, anyway. But Tom saw him—he thinks he's telling the truth." He sighed. "I'm not so sure—maybe he *and* Wade were up there, and he got cold feet this morning. I've got someone hanging about his house to make sure he doesn't go underground like Wade."

Judy looked back at her notes. "Sandwell, acting on Sklodowski's information, went to the boating lake at ten past six, where he found the body of Julia Mitchell."

"Right. And we now know that she left Donald Mitchell's house at half past seven, went with him to the boating lake, where they had a row, left and went to the Shorts, where they arrived at about twenty past eight."

"How far is it from the boating lake to the Shorts' house?"

"About five minutes in a car," Lloyd said.

"What were they doing there all that time? Having this row?"

"Well—the Shorts think there might be rather more to it than that. It seems Donald wasn't obeying all the commandments." Lloyd took from his pocket the pre-wrapped and sterilised sandwiches that the canteen had sold him, and began unenthusiastically to unwrap them. "They think it was Julia giving him the brush-off now that she was rich."

"Lovely—what with that and Wade being Mrs. Mitchell's fancy man—still. Go on."

"She stayed at the Shorts for less than two minutes, because Mitchell called her names. As she was leaving, Wade offered to drive her back—she wasn't too keen on that, apparently, but he persuaded her."

"Did she know Wade?"

"No. That was the first time they'd met."

"Just as well," said Judy dryly.

Lloyd bit into his plastic sandwich. "You can only tell by the colour whether it's ham or cheese," he complained, opening it gingerly to see what colour this one was. It was pink, with a tiny white border. "Donald Mitchell stayed at the Shorts until after eleven, because of the storm. Though," he said, thoughtfully, "Elaine Short did tell me to ask Helen Mitchell where she was—apparently she couldn't be raised."

"They've found her clothes, by the way," Judy said. "And the preliminary medical report confirms the doctor's theory that there was no sexual assault. It says, in fact, that the clothes were removed with care."

Lloyd sighed. "Blows my theory, though," he said. Wade, turned rapist and killer by the death of his wife in a car crash for which he felt responsible. Nice and neat. Then he brightened. "No *assault*, but—"

"No sexual activity before or after death," Judy quoted. "See for yourself."

Frowning, Lloyd read the short, much qualified report. If there was no sexual activity, why didn't she have any clothes on?

"It wasn't that hot," he said. "Unless—" But he decided to keep it to himself for the moment.

"Unless what?" Judy asked eagerly.

He leant over conspiratorially. "I'm not sure. I'll tell you later." He laughed at her aggravated expression. "A man's got to retain some mystery," he said, with a toss of the head.

Donald slept in the chair, the Observer having slipped from his grasp to the floor. He hadn't eaten lunch, but he looked better than he had, Helen thought, as his deep regular breathing filled the room. The wind moved into the fresh to strong league, catching the window which wasn't fastened properly, and as she closed it, Donald woke and stretched.

"That's better," he said, instantly awake, as he always was. He picked up the paper and folded it. "Has Martin told you about last night?" he asked.

Helen recognised the attempt at a casual question. It was the tone of voice he used when he thought she might have found something out. This would be the explanation, the thing that made it all right.

"I haven't spoken to Martin," she said. "I had a word with Elaine, but she didn't say anything."

"She will."

Helen sat down. "Go on," she said.

"When we left here, we went up to the café—she said she wanted to see it before she decided finally one way or the other."

Helen nodded. Why the big build-up? She knew that already. "You told the policeman you'd had an argument with her," she said.

Donald sighed. "That was an understatement."

"Oh?" Helen prepared herself to listen to yet another of Donald's complicated lies. He seemed to think that as long as he included imaginative little details, no one would ever suspect.

"We had a flaming row," he told her, a little sheepishly. "It seems ridiculous now."

"About the boating lake?" Helen tried to keep the scepticism out of her voice, but she could hear it herself.

"Yes!" Donald said, hurt surprise registering automatically. "About the boating lake—I told you it was ridiculous." He picked up his almost untouched whisky. "She was coming into all that money—we haven't even sorted out how much the estate's worth yet—and she was insisting on *selling* that place to the Council." He downed his drink, and rose to get another. Helen nursed her gin and tonic, mindful of Donald's warning about keeping her wits about her for the police.

"Why didn't Charles put it in his will if he wanted to donate it to the town?"

"Search me. I didn't do his will, if you remember."

She remembered all right. Charles had found it easier to go to the solicitor who handled the Mitchell Development business in London, and Donald was most put out.

"What made you think you could change her mind?"

"Oh, I don't know. I just thought I'd have one last go at making her see reason."

"Why did it turn into a row?" Helen normally accepted his stories at face value, said "yes, dear" and got on with her life. But Julia hadn't seemed in the least interested in the boating lake. The whole thing was just an excuse, and now he was embroidering it.

"It got personal. By the time we got to Martin's, we were calling each other names."

Helen was sure it had got personal. She raised her eyebrows slightly, but didn't speak.

"She couldn't have cared less about the boating lake," he said, as though he could read her mind. "It was just an excuse—something I wanted her to do. Something Charles would have wanted her to do. So she wasn't going to do it."

Why? Why did he always keep up the pretence? Why did they play this game of lies, excuses, plausible stories? Year after year they had done it. He told them, she listened, and they both knew he was lying. She had come to the conclusion that he had affairs purely for the mental exercise of lying his way out of being caught. The boating lake was just an excuse, all right—an excuse to have Julia there, under his own roof, making the game more challenging than ever.

And now the initial shock had worn off, her death didn't

really seem to have touched him at all. It certainly hadn't spoiled the game.

"You want me to come too?" Judy looked at her desk. There was the fire at the school during the holidays—almost certainly arson; there was the purse stealer at Blend-vend, and she was supposed to be preparing a crime prevention leaflet for the Chamber of Commerce, with particular reference to dissuading shoplifters—one point on which was that they mustn't call them shoplifters. Shop thefts, shop thieves. She had to give evidence on Thursday, and there was a lot of paperwork to do on that . . . she stopped thinking about it. "All right," she said.

On the way to the Sklodowskis', they tossed theories backwards and forwards like a tennis ball.

"What was Paul Thingy doing in the woods, anyway?" Judy asked.

"Answering the call of nature," Lloyd said.

"Do you mean having a pee or bird-watching?"

"The former."

The car picked up speed on the road out to Homewood, where Stansfield's well-heeled residents chose to live. The made-to-measure houses with their swimming pools and tennis courts—much used this summer, for a change—passed in procession.

"Took a hell of a long time over it, didn't he?" Judy remarked, as she turned into Purcell Avenue.

"Couldn't start his motorbike," Lloyd shrugged. "I thought he might be a Peeping Tom, but Tom—our Tom," he said, with a laugh, "says he'd bet money that he's got nothing to do with it. Says we'll know why when we see him."

The car drew into the tarmacked driveway of a Spanish hacienda, whitewashed, pink tiled, and shuttered.

"You did say they were Polish?" Judy asked, as they got out of the car, and negotiated the shining new motorbike in the drive.

"Something like that," Lloyd said, walking back to where

42

P.C. Alderton waited. "You can get back to work now," he said. "We've arrived with the thumb-screws."

Mrs. Sklodowska was clearing away the remains of Sunday lunch when they went in, having been heartily welcomed by Paul's father, a square, fair man in looks, and almost certainly in temperament, Judy thought. His eyes, even bluer than Lloyd's, looked anxious.

"Alice, this is the police. The other car is not here now." He turned to Judy. "You will understand—she not like the car out there so long. I told her—they don't know Paul. He has killed this lady, they think."

"No, no we don't," Judy said. "But we can't take chances."

"I tell her that."

Sklodowski's command of the English language was total, but his speech was still peppered with vees, and his syntax was a little eccentric.

"This car is just a car," he assured his wife, who tucked a strand of greying hair back into her unfashionable bun.

"I'm sorry," she said. "But it did bother me a bit. Paul only reported it—I mean, you don't really think he had anything to do with it, do you?"

Lloyd smiled. "Well, we'd like to talk to him. How old is he, Mrs. Sklodowska?"

Judy could feel his smugness in remembering the feminine of the name—especially since Mrs. S. was English, and that much more likely to be impressed.

"He's just turned eighteen." She frowned. "Do you want to see him alone?"

"Not necessarily," he said. "We'll see how it goes."

Paul was called down from his room, and entered shyly, another version of his father. They all got themselves reasonably comfortably seated before Lloyd began.

"Paul—my sergeant tells me that you were on your way to work when you came in this morning. Where do you work?"

"Mitchell's," he said. "I was on six to two."

"Why did you wait until this morning?"

43

Paul moved uncomfortably. "I told him. I thought I would be wasting your time. But then it worried me all night, and I decided to come in and tell you."

Judy looked at him. She could see what Tom meant. He seemed to be a nice-looking, well-built, normal young man. Peeping Toms usually gave off vibrations of failure, and Paul didn't. And yet she didn't think he was telling the truth.

"What else did you think might have happened?" she asked.

Paul looked politely puzzled.

"I mean—when you saw the car come back with just the man in it—what reasons did you give yourself? What did you think might be the perfectly simple explanation?"

He looked at Lloyd, then back at her, and mumbled something she couldn't catch.

"Sorry? What did you say?"

"I thought she might have dropped something—she might just have been bending down, and I didn't see her. Or he might just have been dropping her off there—a shortcut or something. But it didn't seem very likely."

"Anyway," Lloyd said, smiling benignly at him. "You took his number, just in case. Do you know whose number it was?"

"No."

"Are you sure? You didn't recognise the car?"

"No. It was a Cortina, that's all."

"What colour?" Judy asked, remembering her conversation with Mrs. Marsden.

"I can't remember," he said, his face becoming more miserable by the minute.

"How do you know it was the same car that you saw going up?"

He shrugged. "It looked the same."

"But it could have been a different car?" Lloyd asked.

Paul shrugged again.

His mother and father did seem a great deal more anxious to help than Paul did. Judy found herself hoping that he would

44

become more forthcoming. She didn't like the idea of taking him in for questioning from under the noses of his parents.

"Got any brothers or sisters, Paul?" Lloyd was asking, as though he were changing the subject.

"Two brothers," Paul answered.

"Older or younger?" Judy joined in.

"Older."

Lloyd laughed. "I'll bet they led you a dog's life, didn't they?"

"No." Paul looked uncomprehendingly at him.

"Mine did. My big brother—he still bullies me if he gets the chance!" Lloyd laughed. Lloyd hadn't got a big brother.

"My brothers are a lot older than me," Paul said. "They were almost grown up when I was born."

Mrs. Sklodowska was nodding vigorously in confirmation.

"So you were spoiled rotten by them, were you?" Judy tried.

Paul smiled shyly. "I expect so," he said.

"Let you have everything your own way, did they?" Lloyd was still being jocular.

"I don't know," Paul said. "They were always sending me for things—to the shops, or upstairs, or next door." He laughed a little himself, as he began to relax.

He was a very young eighteen, Judy thought, but that was probably to be expected.

"Helped you with your homework, did they?" Lloyd persisted.

"Sometimes." Paul looked at his father.

"Were you sometimes a bit jealous of them? They were grown up, weren't they? They could do what they liked, and you had to do what you were told."

Paul shook his head. "No, I never minded."

"Have you ever heard of a man called Christopher Wade?" Judy asked.

"No, I don't think so." There wasn't a glimmer of recognition as he answered. Not the merest blink. "Why?" he asked.

45

"Just wondered," Judy said, aware of Mrs. Sklodowska's eyes upon her. "What about friends, Paul? Why weren't you out with your mates on a Saturday night?"

"I don't know." Paul looked under his fair eyebrows at her.

"Girlfriends?" asked Lloyd.

Paul blushed to the roots of his blond hair.

Judy bit her lip slightly, trying to understand the reaction. Why blush? Boys of eighteen sometimes had wives, never mind girlfriends. Why should the question embarrass him?

"Well?" Lloyd said. "Don't tell me you've no girlfriends—a good-looking lad like you?"

"There is a girl," Sklodowski said, interrupting for the first time. "Why do you not answer? She is a nice girl—we have known her a long time. Why do you blush?" He caught his son's arm. "Eh? Why don't you answer?"

Paul took a deep breath. "He's told you," he said. "Diane. Why are you asking about her?"

"Just interested," Judy said. "Why weren't you out with Diane?"

Paul blushed again, but not so painfully this time. "Her dad won't let her," he said.

"What?" Sklodowski stared at him. "What do you mean? Since when?"

Paul shrugged.

"Don't *do* that!" His father hit him gently on the shoulder. "Why does he not let her? What have you done?"

"Nothing!" Paul sighed. "I think it bothers him. Because you got on and he didn't. I don't know why. But he said she's not to see me."

"What age is Diane?" Lloyd asked.

"Seventeen. It's not long to wait until he can't tell her who to see. We don't mind waiting." Paul waited patiently for more questions.

"Why were you in the wood for so long?" Judy asked. "You saw the car arrive, and leave—that was half an hour later, you said."

Paul nodded dumbly.

"What were you doing?"

"I've said," Paul muttered. "I couldn't start my bike."

"What's wrong with it?" Lloyd asked. "It's brand new—it was a very warm night—you shouldn't have trouble starting it."

"I don't know!" Paul shouted.

"Did you go up there? Did you go up to see what was going on?"

"What?" The question came from both Paul and his mother.

"You heard," Lloyd said, his voice hard. "Did you want to watch?"

Paul stared at him. "You're joking," he finally said.

"Am I? I thought you must be with that story about the bike."

Paul stood up, and so did Lloyd. Paul was inches taller. "The bike broke down," he said. Anger had made him lose his self-consciousness. Suddenly, he didn't seem so young.

"Why didn't you push it? You're a big lad—Wade's garage is just down the road."

But Paul didn't take the bait that Lloyd was dangling. If he knew that Wade wasn't at the garage, he didn't give himself away.

"Who is this Wade?" he asked. "Why do you keep dragging him—oh! That's whose car I saw—right? So why should I know him?"

Lloyd walked away from him, over to the window. "Oh, no," he said. "I don't think you know him. At first I did. I thought maybe you knew the car, and didn't want to tell. But now I've got it. You went up to have a look, didn't you? And that's when you saw him. And it frightened you, so you ran away. That's it, isn't it?"

Paul looked at Judy. "It was nothing like that," he said mildly.

Judy allowed herself a smile. "Then tell us what it was like."

* * *

Chris awoke with a start, staring at a damp green wall. For a second, he had no idea where he was, but then the unwelcome memories flooded back. He could see faces—Julia's, pinched and frightened, phone in her hand to call the police. He'd only been trying to apologise, see if she was hurt. She didn't have to do that. He'd tried to explain to Helen—he could see her face, worried and loving. He could vaguely see Donald's. Worried, asking him over and over again what he'd done. She shouldn't have said those things—she shouldn't. He remembered the garage, and the bottle of whisky that he'd found. Whisky to try to blot out the memory, but it hadn't worked. Carrie's familiar face was there. It had all come rushing back to him as he drove away from the wood. Carrie, lying in the street in the rain, covered with someone's plastic mac. The rain teeming down, running off the coat into the road. Police cars, their lights flashing blue through the steady downpour; the ambulance, siren braying, inching its way through the Christmas crowds who couldn't help and wouldn't leave. And he didn't have a scratch. Nothing—nothing wrong with him at all. He had drunk the whisky to make it go away, but it had stayed, and he'd let Helen down.

Now, he felt sick. He had a splitting headache, but he could think more clearly. Julia was dead. He didn't care, that much he did know. But someone else must have come along and killed her, because she was alive and kicking when he left. He tried to think of what they'd done. He'd taken her up there, gone in, tried to talk to her, had a row. He remembered thinking that she must be picking rows with everyone, because she and Donald were having a row when they arrived at Elaine's. She couldn't have died—not from what he did. No one dies, not like that. Not after they've threatened to phone the police and hurled abuse at you. Oh, that was just being stupid. Of course she didn't die from anything he did. Someone went up there and killed her.

God knows, there were probably enough people who wanted to.

* * *

The teams of men moved out, widening the area that they were searching. The cameramen were being allowed in now, and they filmed the spot where the girl had been found, and the outside of the building that was still sealed off. Flashes supplemented the daylight, as the press got their photographs of the police searching every inch of the woodland. Reporters hovered, having to make do with press statements until they could find a real live policeman to talk to, because right now they were all too busy.

So they grumbled about the weather, and their accommodation, and the fact that their expenses wouldn't cover their expenditure, what with the hotel costing the bloody earth and it was all right for lorry drivers, they could sleep in the cab. And they sat gloomily in their cars, or on the still damp grass until they discovered that it was still damp, and they watched the people who were working, and wished that they were, or that the pubs were open.

They wouldn't even say who they were looking for, though they obviously all knew. They'd heard the rumours, of course, but you can't print rumours. You can mention the odd disappearance of one Christopher Wade, garage proprietor, which you just happen to have picked up while you were in the area. Is he another victim? But it wasn't as good as coming right out with it. Widow's Death—Local Businessman Sought. Come to that—why hadn't they found him?

Will Lakeside Killer Strike Again?

CHAPTER FOUR

STRIKES, TROUBLE IN THE MIDDLE EAST, TROUBLE IN Northern Ireland; they took second place to trouble here in Stansfield, which had caught the attention of the national news, as Helen watched, waiting to hear what was happening. The policeman hadn't come back; not yet, anyway. Donald, less interested, was on the phone to someone, arranging to go to London tomorrow.

The familiar music of the early evening news, opening with the pictures she had already seen in her mind. The police searching the wood; the lake, looking dark and cold as the wind ruffled its surface.

"The beauty spot where early this morning the body of thirty-five year old Julia Mitchell was found. 'We know who we are looking for,' says Superintendent James Randall.

"Good Evening." The newsreader smiled the serious smile that newsreaders keep for these occasions. *"Police have issued a description of the man they wish to interview in connection with the murder of Julia Mitchell, widow of property developer Charles Mitchell. Mrs. Mitchell's body was found early this morning, near a boating lake in Stansfield, where she was visiting relatives. Mel Brown has this report."*

The camera moved round the closed café, showing closeups of the windows and the door, for no good reason. The reporter walked up to the camera. *"This is the café where it is believed that Julia Mitchell met her death. Mrs. Mitchell*

*owned this popular beauty spot, and was in Stansfield to
negotiate its sale. She was staying . . .''* Here the camera
swivelled round to show the curve of the road, and the houses
at the far end. *" . . . just down the road there, with her
brother-in-law and his wife, Donald and Helen Mitchell. The
Mitchells were not available for comment this morning.''* The
camera moved back to the café, and the reporter. *"Superintendent James Randall, who is leading the murder hunt,
said in a statement this afternoon 'We are looking for a particular man whom we know was with Mrs. Mitchell yesterday
evening, and who may be a vital witness. We are not at present releasing his name.' ''*

Helen breathed a sigh of relief. Somehow, if his name
wasn't mentioned, it didn't seem so bad.

The newsreader appeared again. *"The police have, however, issued a description of the man, who is six feet tall,
with dark straight hair and brown eyes. He was last seen
wearing brown corduroy trousers, and a light brown shirt.
Police appeal to anyone who may have seen him or Mrs.
Mitchell, who had shoulder-length blonde hair, and was
wearing a denim skirt and jacket, to come forward. Thorpe
Wood, and the boating lake itself, is a popular spot for court-
ing couples, and the police emphasise that any information
will be treated in the strictest confidence.''* Then the film of
the police searching the woods again. *"Teams of police are
combing the area for clues, and it is thought that her attacker
may be hiding out there. Tracker dogs may be used in the
search.*

"And now for the rest of today's news . . .''

Helen didn't listen to the rest of today's news.

"The bike wouldn't start."

Lloyd looked sideways at Judy, and she took over.

"How long did it take to start? I mean—it did start eventually, didn't it?"

He nodded.

"How long?"

The evening sun slanted into the room, landing like a spotlight on Paul. "I don't know. About ten minutes, I suppose."

"But you were there for half an hour," Judy said. "You should tell your mum to give you All-Bran—half an hour! That's no fun, in amongst the nettles."

"Could I beg a cup of tea, Mrs. Sklodowska?" Lloyd asked. He did want one; the plastic sandwich seemed to be lodged half way down. And he wanted her to go, to see if that made Paul any more co-operative.

Alice Sklodowska went off to comply with his request, and Lloyd caught Paul's father's eye. He looked back steadily, his gentle features placid, secure in the knowledge that his son had done nothing wrong.

"Paul," Judy said. "Whatever it is you're not telling us isn't worth it."

Lloyd rubbed his eyes. They had been here over two hours, and they were no further forward. He decided to go on the attack again.

"All right," he said. "You'd better come back with us—the Superintendent will want to see you."

Paul looked alarmed, as he was meant to. "What for? I just reported it."

"No, you didn't. I don't think you're a Peeping Tom—I think you went up there after you saw the car leave. You wondered about the girl, so you went up there, and you found her—on her own. What happened, Paul—did you lose your temper? Don't worry, it'll probably just be manslaughter—particularly if she led you on—did she lead you on?"

Paul stared at him, horrified, as his mother came in with the tea.

"Look—my son, he reported—" Sklodowski began, but he didn't get a chance to finish the sentence.

"Yes!" Lloyd said sharply. "He reported it. He told us where to go and find a dead body, and we found one. Come on, son—get your coat."

"But he did not kill this girl—he's just a boy!"

Lloyd looked over at Paul, who still sat, wide-eyed with fear. "No he's not—look at him. He's a big lad. Strong. She

52

wasn't very strong, was she, Paul? It would be easy to strangle her."

Paul jumped to his feet. "I was never anywhere near her! It wasn't me—it was the man in the car! I didn't see anything—I've told you what I saw. Diane can tell you—she was there!"

Lloyd sat back. "Diane," he said. "Is that what this was all about? Diane?" He picked up his tea, and took two deliberate sips before speaking again. "We," he said, in his deepest, threatening, but well-modulated tones, "we have just spent all afternoon here because of Diane? Because Sir Galahad here wanted to protect her reputation?"

"No—it was—yes." Paul hung his head, and muttered, almost to himself. "She made me promise," he said. "She didn't want me to tell anyone about it at all. Because her dad would find out where she'd been."

Lloyd contented himself with looking contemptuously at him. "Right," he said briskly. "Her name and address, please."

"MacPherson," Sklodowski said quickly. "Diane MacPherson—she lives on the Queen's Estate, but she's a very nice girl. They lived next door to us when she and Paul were—" he indicated very small children. His fractured English seemed to be mending nicely, Lloyd noticed, and then he realised what name Sklodowski had given.

"MacPherson?" he asked. "Not Matt MacPherson's girl?"

"Yes—you know Matt?"

"Yes—I worked with him once," Lloyd said. "Diane's seventeen, is she? I thought she was about nine." He laughed.

"It is 39 Victoria Street," Sklodowski continued, glaring at his son. "No wonder Matt won't let you see her!" he shouted, aiming an ineffectual blow at Paul, and missing. "It's flat 5," he added.

Lloyd and Judy made for the door.

"Don't get her into trouble," Paul pleaded.

"You're more likely to do that than I am," Lloyd said. "We'll need a statement. I'll let you know when."

Out on the Spanish-style porch, he spoke to Paul's father. "Don't be too hard on him—we were all young once."

"Teenagers!" Sklodowski said with as much disgust as he could muster. "When I was his age we were too busy trying to stay alive to get up to mischief in the woods!"

Despite the talk, Lloyd didn't imagine that Sklodowski had ever been hard on Paul in his life, and he didn't suppose he would start now. Diane MacPherson—well, well. He must be getting old.

It was getting dark, and Chris could venture further afield. He had had one or two furtive excursions outside his shelter when forced to by bodily need, but now it was too dark for them to be searching, and he could find something to eat.

The fresh, pine-scented breeze seemed like heaven after the foul-smelling cell, and he limped away towards the old wood where the wind would have brought down some apples. He tried to work out the last time he had eaten, but he kept forgetting which day was which. It must have been Saturday morning, because he didn't have lunch. Had Elaine given him anything? No, because they'd eaten early. They were expecting Donald and Julia round to discuss the boating lake.

Why hadn't he just dropped her there, like she'd asked? Oh no, he had to take her to the door. She'd left something up there, she said. Just drop her here, she could walk the rest of the way. She'd be all right, you could see the house from here. But she hadn't left anything. She'd tricked him in there with a stupid lie, and he still couldn't see why. God damn it, she hadn't killed herself. Or had she? People did, after all. His mind toyed with that idea for a moment, but it was too fantastic. Why would she want—? For a moment, it did seem to be the answer. She hadn't wanted him to run her back, because she intended doing away with herself. She got rid of him, and did it. Simple. Simple, except that the police were asking about him. Still—it might just be to see if he knew why she'd killed herself. Maybe she drowned herself in the boating lake. Maybe they weren't really looking for him, not like that.

But as he dragged his way back to his hide-out, he knew that he was whistling in the dark. He'd seen all the police cars—even heard a couple of policemen who got too close for comfort. Helen had lied for him. And Julia couldn't have been described as suicidal. When she had admitted that she hadn't left anything at all, said she just wanted to be with him—he had wondered, briefly, what was in store for him. His wildest fantasy would not have included Julia's being dead by morning and his being hunted like a wounded animal.

He crawled back in as darkness began to fall, and released his small load of hard, unappetising apples. He'd give himself up. Even if he couldn't work it out, he'd give himself up soon. Tomorrow. Soon, anyway.

Queen's Estate wasn't far from Homewood, but it could have been a million miles away. The car was parked as inconspicuously as possible by garages, whose defaced and damaged doors no longer closed, and which rarely housed anything as valuable as a car. The six doors presented an opportunity to one paint-spray wielder to inscribe MANUTD upon them in red paint.

"The theory is," Lloyd said as they walked past, "that Manchester United has a greater following than any other football club because the fans only need to remember six letters."

"You know this girl, do you?" Judy asked.

"I thought I did—but she's grown up a bit since I saw her last."

Judy laughed. "Peter must be about her age, isn't he?"

"Yes—he'll be eighteen in January. I wonder if he's getting up to mischief in the woods. I suppose he is—I don't see that much of him now."

"Does Linda still come round?"

"Sometimes. But she's growing up too. I'm glad she doesn't come so often—she must be getting over it."

They negotiated some broken bricks which lay around for no good reason, and arrived at the surprisingly intact glass door of the flats. On the step, in the same neat, red lettering, was the greeting SHIT.

"My mother was telling me that she came across two schoolgirls the other day—neat white stockings, blue skirts and blazers, satchels, hats—the lot, demurely writing 'Mrs. Masters is a shit' on the wall with a magic marker," Judy said, thinking that perhaps it was just that Magic Markers and paint spray hadn't been invented when she was a demure schoolgirl.

Lloyd shrugged, and they climbed the stairs to the top flat.

"He's always lived here," he said. "He thinks there ought to be pockets of resistance."

"How come it got like this?"

"Nobody really knows. Every now and then they try to brighten its image a bit, but it doesn't really work. Though it isn't as bad as it used to be—there are quite a lot of people who haven't run away. I think it was a sort of vicious circle. One or two bad lots moved in, and we started keeping a special eye on the area. Because we were there, other people wouldn't move in. Still," he said philosophically, "you name me a town that hasn't got a seedy quarter. They just happen."

The door was opened by a pale, thin woman of indeterminate age, with short, mousy hair and a smile of half recognition.

"It's Lloyd, isn't it? It's years since I've seen you! Matt! Matt—look who's here!"

Everyone called him Lloyd. Judy lived in hopes of someone calling him Algernon or Dafydd, or whatever name his parents had landed him with, but no one ever did. And he wouldn't even tell her when she admitted that her middle name was Cornelia.

"Come in, please," Mrs. MacPherson continued. "The place is a mess—you should have said you were coming."

She stood aside, and Lloyd and Judy stepped in, to be greeted by Matt, whose Scottish accent had not been one whit diminished by living in the east of England for over twenty years.

"How are you doing?" Matt asked, pumping Lloyd's hand. "And who's this? You've been keeping her a secret."

Judy felt uncomfortable, because they so obviously thought it was a social visit.

"It's been far too long," Mrs. MacPherson said. She had an accentless voice that could have come from anywhere.

"I'm afraid it's business, Polly. We can't stay. This is Detective Sergeant Hill, Matt—Polly."

Matt gave Judy an appreciative look. "There were no detectives like you in my day," he said. "All I got were hairy beer drinkers like this one." He jerked a finger at Lloyd. "And Welsh, as if it wasn't bad enough!"

"Matt was on the force," Lloyd explained.

"Aye, but I never had the brains—I couldn't afford it," Matt said, and laughed.

"Are you working now?" Lloyd asked.

Matt shook his head. "There's nothing. But there's some sort of an electronics place supposed to be starting up soon— I'll see if they're looking for security men. 'Sorry, but we're bringing our staff with us.' That's what I'll get." He had put a high-pitched, mincing accent for the quote, and employed it again. " 'Just leave your name with us, Mr. MacPherson— we'll bear you in mind.' They're all the same, these places. But I'll take nightwatchman if it's going—I don't want to be idle—see these kids? Half of them are scared to work. But they can get them for nothing."

By now the group had progressed into the living room, a quietly furnished, airy room, quite unlike its exterior surroundings. "Mind you, we're all right for now—I've got my redundancy. And if Diane gets that job she's after on the paper—" He broke off. "Here, where's that beer I brought back?"

"On the sideboard," Mrs. MacPherson's voice came from the kitchen.

"Oh here they are. Will you have a beer?"

"Thanks, I will." Lloyd said.

"Business, you said?"

"Yes," Lloyd said, slightly hesitantly. "Is Diane in?"

"She's in her bedroom reading. She's forever reading, that one—I think she must have read half the library by now." He paused. "Why? What's she been up to?"

"Nothing," Lloyd assured him. "It's just that we were given her name as being a possible witness."

"What to?" he asked, suspiciously.

"Nothing, probably. You know what these things are like. It's about this girl—young woman—who was found in Thorpe Wood. Do you know about it?"

Matt looked incredulous. "Of course I know about it. It's been all over the news—what's she got to do with it?"

"Nothing at all. But we think she might have been around there last night." Lloyd paused for a moment. "If we could have a word with her," he said. "If she was there, she might have seen something."

"What would she be doing there?" Matt's dark brows almost met.

"Probably just passing," Judy said lightly. "But she might remember something—a car, or whatever."

"It's just that someone thought they saw her," Lloyd tried.

"On her own?" Matt opened one of the beer cans with a small explosion of froth.

"Couldn't tell you," Lloyd lied valiantly.

"She'd better've been."

"Could I have a word with her?" Judy asked, as though it didn't really matter whether she did or not. She shook her head with a smile at the proffered can of beer.

"Just go through," Matt said. "She's used to the law tramping all over the house. That's her door there." He indicated the door to the right of the kitchen.

"Who was she with? A boy?" Matt asked, as Judy left. "If she was with that Paul What's-his-name, you'll not be the only one having a word with her. I told her—I'm not having that."

"I've no idea, Matt. It was just her name we were given," Lloyd said, getting himself into deeper water than ever.

"Do you know what her mother found in her bedroom?"

Judy by this time had heard "come in" in a puzzled voice coming from the other side of the bedroom door, and had to guess the answer.

Diane was stretched out on the bed, reading, as her father had predicted, and looked up curiously when Judy walked in. Her mother's face and her father's colouring were an interesting combination; her brown eyes appraised Judy, a slight frown drawing her eyebrows together.

"I'm Judy Hill. I'm sorry to barge in on you, but your dad said it would be all right. I'm a detective sergeant with Stansfield police."

"Oh. Did you work with my dad?"

"No—but the inspector did. They're having a beer now." Judy looked round the small, neat room. "May I sit down?"

Diane slid her legs off the bed to make room, and Judy sat. "It's about last night," she said. "We've spoken to Paul."

The girl stiffened slightly. "What about last night?"

"Do you know that someone was found dead in Thorpe Wood last night? A woman?"

The girl clearly did not. "The woman we saw?" she asked, in a whisper.

"Yes," said Judy. "I hope that makes you feel a bit more like telling us what you saw?"

"Of course it does! I wouldn't have—I thought he was making a big thing of it." She shook her head. "If I'd thought for a moment that—"

"Let's have your version, then."

Diane looked up sharply. "My *version*?" she repeated. "What do you mean, my version?"

"Your account, then. But it will be a version, whether you like it or not—no two people see exactly the same things, notice exactly the same things. We know what Paul saw, and now I want to hear what you saw."

Diane pulled her legs up underneath her. "Does my dad know where I was?" she asked.

Judy sighed. "Paul said there had been trouble—he very nearly got himself arrested pretending he was there on his own."

"He would." She didn't look entirely grateful for Paul's efforts on her behalf. "What have you told my dad?"

"Just that you were seen in the area. Not where you were, or who you were with."

"He'll find out though, won't he?" She made a face. "I'll have to tell him before he reads it in the paper." She seemed to have resigned herself to that; she faced Judy brightly. "Go on then—what do you want to know?"

"What you saw."

"Right. A car drove up the lane—it's a pathway, really, and stopped just opposite us because they had to open the gate. It drove on, and when it came back later, Paul said only the man was in it. There had been a girl in the passenger seat when it went in there."

"How do you know?"

Diane looked at her more in sorrow than in anger. "How do you suppose? I saw her, that's how."

Judy took out her notebook, and made a production out of consulting it. "What time was this, Diane?"

"Half past eight," she said immediately. "When the car came."

"It was dark then, wasn't it?"

"Yes—I know what you're going to say. But when he got out to open the gate, the car light came on. And I could see her as well as I can see you now. She was blonde—good-looking, considering."

"Considering what? Her great age?"

Diane laughed. "Sorry. She was about your age, I'd think." She thought for a moment. "But I didn't just mean that—she looked a bit, well—scared."

Judy gave Diane the old-fashioned look with which she could infuriate Lloyd on one of his flights of fancy.

"She did! It's not because I know what happened now—I noticed at the time, really, I did!"

Judy made a note to come back to that later. "Then what?" she asked.

"Two minutes past nine, the car came back down. Paul was over by the bike—his motor bike, and so he was quite close to it. And he came back and told me that the girl wasn't in it. He started to worry about it, and wanted to go up and check, but I stopped him." She dropped her eyes. "I didn't know," she said. "I'd never have just gone away if I'd thought anything like that had happened. But Paul—he's a big kid, really—you'll know that if you've talked to him—and he likes making mysteries. You know, UFOs and the Bermuda Triangle and all that sort of thing. He'd be just as likely to believe the Martians had got her."

"You didn't believe him?"

Diane slid off the bed, and tried to put her feelings into words several times before she actually succeeded.

"I believed him," she said finally, looking out of the window, her back to Judy. "I believed he hadn't seen her. But I didn't think for a minute that anything had happened to her— I thought she'd just bent down, or it was a short cut to where she lived, and he'd dropped her off there."

Judy smiled. "These were your theories, were they?"

"They weren't theories! I just didn't think—" she broke off. "I was wrong. I'm sorry." She turned towards Judy, her face worried. "Was she—I mean, if we'd gone up, would she have been all right?"

"I doubt it very much, but we don't know exactly when she died yet. She was strangled—I expect whoever did it made sure."

Diane sat down again, her face pale. "That's all there is," she said. "Paul had taken his number. I thought he might ring up, not give his name—but I should have known he couldn't do that."

"Did you see the driver?"

"Not really. Just a man—I couldn't describe him. I saw her, that's all."

61

"What were you and Paul doing when this car arrived, and left?"

Diane raised her eyebrows. "What do you think?"

"Well," Judy said. "That is what I thought. But if you were—let's say otherwise engaged—how come you know exactly when the car came, exactly when it left—what she looked like right down to the expression on her face?"

"It's got nothing to do with you," Diane said sulkily.

"No, it hasn't, normally." Judy stood, since standing seemed to carry rather more authority than perching on the edge of Diane's bed. "And if no one had been found dead, it would have continued to have nothing to do with me. But Mrs. Mitchell was strangled. And you and Paul have told me what you saw." She stepped closer to the bed. "And what you saw seems to have been a murderer arriving with his victim, and leaving without her. Which is rather important evidence—would you agree?"

Diane didn't answer, or look at her.

"When you are giving evidence in court, the defence will want to know how come you noticed so much, when you could have been forgiven for not noticing anything. And I want to know now."

"It was awful," Diane said, addressing her pillow. "We'd never—" She looked up then, with a quick smile. "Well, not awful, but not very good. I was frightened someone would see us, and it was too hot, and uncomfortable, and—" She gave a little, nervous laugh. "When that car came, I nearly died of fright—and then I thought it was coming back again, because it stopped half way along—I heard its brakes. I didn't want to do it then, but I'd said." She looked back at her pillow then, safe from any reaction. "So we stayed." Her face coloured. "Will I have to tell people this in court?"

"You might have to," Judy said, coming back and sitting on the bed. "It depends how much other evidence we get." She touched the girl's shoulder. "I'm sorry," she said. "But they will want to know how you could be so sure of the times."

"I'm supposed to be in by half past nine." She stared hard

62

at the pillow. "I kept asking Paul the time—I was trying to get out of it," she said, embarrassed. "I made him show me his watch when the car came."

She anticipated Judy's next question.

"It lights up—you know." She paused. "And then afterwards I'd got all bits of dead grass on me, and I was trying to get them off. He was over at the bike, and he couldn't get it started, and I didn't dare come home late, not after—" She looked up. "I asked him what time it was, and he said it was two minutes past nine. And that's when the car came back."

It had been difficult, and Judy gave her a little pat. "Did you see the car leave?" she asked.

"Yes, but I was too far away to see who was in it."

"Thank you. We will want you to make a formal statement, but you won't have to put all that in it." She smiled. "Paul seems a nice lad—why doesn't your father want you to see him?"

Diane closed her eyes. "It's stupid," she said. "We've always gone around together. I just thought that if it was getting serious, well, I should—you know. I went on the pill, and my mum found them." She opened her eyes. "She told him, and he went mad. I told him nothing had happened, but he didn't believe me." She shrugged. "So on Saturday I thought—why not?"

"We won't say any more to your dad than we have to," Judy said. "But you'd better tell him something before he finds out some other way."

"Yes." Diane wasn't really listening.

"And don't worry," Judy said, giving a little wink. "It gets better with practice."

Diane looked up. "It couldn't get much worse," she said, with a wry smile. "It *was* awful."

Donald sipped his coffee. "That was a lovely meal," he said to Helen, who always found more solace in cooking than in eating, and hadn't really done hers justice. "It deserves a brandy," he said. "Would you like one?"

"Yes please. You don't think that policeman will be back now do you?"

"No." Donald consulted his watch. "It's almost ten o'clock. Anyway, a brandy will hardly knock you sideways." He poured generous brandies and handed one to Helen. "I don't quite know how to say this," he said. "It doesn't seem the right time, but I don't suppose there can be a right time when something like this happens."

Helen, immediately alarmed, almost choked on her first sip. "What? Has something else happened?"

"Yes," Donald said. He really didn't know how to put it. The only way was straight out. "I don't suppose you knew— I only know because I'm his executor. It's about Charles's will, really. I only thought of it as I came in after seeing Julia. We're rich, Helen. We're very rich."

Helen took another drink while his words sank in. "Because Julia's dead?" she asked.

Donald nodded. "Charles left Julia a great deal of money," he said, "which is hers—I mean, it'll go to her father, or whoever has a better claim. But the bulk of the estate was in trust."

Helen frowned. "Why?"

"It's not unusual—I'd have advised him the same way. You see, he made the will—what—when did they get married? Five years ago? Six?"

"Five—last March."

"He made it when they got married, and he expected there to be children. To be honest, I think that's why he married her, despite all the comments."

"Mostly from you," Helen reminded him.

"I know, I know. But it did invite comment. I really believe he thought she was expecting his baby. I don't mean he wouldn't have married her otherwise, but she might not have found it too easy."

"You mean she tricked him?"

"Quite," Donald said. "And when he made the will, he assumed children. And so he left her very well off, but he left the rest of the estate to any children of the marriage.

He hated all that, you know. It was all I could do to get him to make a will in the first place, and then he had to change it all.'' He could see Charles making a nice, general all-purpose will when he got married, so that he wouldn't have to keep coming back to change it.

"If there were no children,'' he carried on, "then the money was to be held in trust for Julia—in other words, she couldn't use it without the say-so of the trustees, and they were his solicitor and the bank. So that she wouldn't do any-thing silly with it.''

"So what happens now that Julia's dead?'' Helen asked. "How do we end up with it?''

"If Julia died, it was to come to me—just that. Not held in trust—he presumably thought I wouldn't do anything too silly. If I predeceased Julia, which at the time would have seemed more than likely, then it had to go to the boys, and so on. Keeping it in the family.''

"So you get it now?''

Donald nodded. "When I went up to see his solicitor, I read that bit, but I just laughed. It was so like Charles, cov-ering every eventuality he could think of with one great big complicated will. When I remembered, I rang Harper to check. And it's true,'' he said. "We're very rich.'' He'd leave the rest until later.

The wind whistled through the trees, moving their branches, filling the air with rustling and sighing. The wood, black and shifting, looked like a wood where someone could die.

The lake, breaking the reflection of the stars into a thou-sand pieces as the water rippled and turned, looked like a bad place for ducks. But the ducks bobbed and weaved on the water, grimly seeing the night out.

The café stood dark and empty, its door nailed up, its secrets given up.

All, that is, except one.

CHAPTER FIVE

SERGEANT JACK WOODFORD KNOCKED AND CAME in. "Good evening," he said to Judy, then looked across at Lloyd, who was stifling a yawn.

"I'm on nightshift," he said. "What's your excuse?"

Lloyd waved a non-committal hand.

"It's quarter to eleven," Jack persisted. "How long have you two been working?"

"Don't work it out," Judy warned. "It'll only make us feel worse than ever."

"I," said Jack, "have taken pity on the defective branch of the police farce, and any minute now coffee should be appearing—" he twisted round and looked at the door. "I don't do it often," he told Judy, his eyes still on the door, "so grovel if you like."

"Can I just be pathetically grateful?"

The door swung open, and the young constable whose name Judy could never remember walked in backwards with three steaming mugs on a tray. "Coffee, sir," he said awkwardly, having completed a tricky turn to face Lloyd.

"You've got it wrong," Jack said. "How many times do I have to tell you? You walk *out* backwards."

Lloyd smiled tiredly, and reached out a hand for his coffee. Jack was very jovial tonight—he didn't know whether he could take it. He didn't know why he was still there. It would be a damn sight easier if they didn't know who they were looking for; he could be doing something then. Something he could get his teeth into. As it was, no one needed him on a door-to-door. Garages and outhouses could get searched without his experienced hand in the matter. All he could do was speak to the people who might be hiding him, and build up the case for the prosecution. And he could do precious little of that until he got the full post mortem results and the forensic reports. Finding him was the only real obstacle, and that just took manpower.

He drank some coffee, burning his mouth. Since they had left the MacPhersons, he and Judy had sorted out the various accounts of what had happened and the only question remaining was why. Why had Wade suddenly turned on a total stranger and strangled her? Why was she naked? Why had her clothes been rolled up into a bundle? Why were her underclothes missing?

"The reason I came in," Jack was saying, "was that we got a telephone call from an anonymous caller saying that Wade had been seen at the Queen's Estate shops. Probably rubbish, but I've sent a car."

"Marvellous how they all know who we're looking for," Lloyd said. "That's the fourth time he's been seen today."

"Why don't you go home? We'll let you know if anything happens, don't worry. You first, then the Super, so long as you don't tell him."

"I'll wait and see how the Queen's thing turns out." He did know why he was staying. He didn't want to go home—he was turning into the kind of policeman who wanted to bring a sleeping bag in and never leave the station. The kind of policeman he swore he'd never be. Or maybe it was because Judy was here—he'd prefer to think that that was why.

"Why are you still here?" he asked Judy. "You've been up even longer than me."

Judy used her eyebrows in a sort of facial shrug. "I thought we'd find him, I suppose," she said. "And it could all be wrapped up tonight."

It didn't sound much more convincing than his reasons.

He wondered—hoped, perhaps, that she was staying because he was there.

"We'll see what happens about this so-called sighting," he said. "Then go."

"Do you want a lift?" Judy asked. "I take it your car's still out of commission?"

"I do, and it is."

Jack left to see how the lads were getting on in Queen's Estate, and came back to report false alarm.

"Right," said Lloyd, putting on his raincoat.

He and Judy walked out of the station into the wind that swirled the rubbish round the car park. Judy's Ford Anglia had seen better days, and Lloyd positively winced at its general condition.

"If you want a lift in a clean car, you'd better ask someone else," she said. "It's the dirt that holds this one together."

He lifted the door slightly before pulling it shut, as he had learned to do now. "Why don't you buy a new one? A newer one, at any rate?" he asked.

"I like this one—it gets me where I'm going, which is more than you can say for yours at the moment." She started the engine, a process not to be undertaken lightly, but which with patience usually worked.

"I just wish I knew why," Lloyd said.

"Why I won't buy a new car?"

He leant back, and rubbed the back of his neck. "Why someone would want to kill someone else that he'd known for about five minutes. I'd like to know if we're dealing with a nutcase or what. You saw her—there certainly wasn't much of a struggle. So he must have taken her by surprise, and just killed her. No rape—no nothing. Just killed her, as though he'd planned it."

Judy moved off. "Maybe he did," she said. "Except that he apparently didn't know the girl from Adam—I think we should look more closely there."

Lloyd nodded. They drove out into the deserted town centre streets. The pubs were closed, and their customers had

68

dispersed. At eleven o'clock, the town could have been innocent of inhabitants.

"Or he just had a brainstorm," Judy suggested.

"But what sort? He took her clothes off—or she did. Why? Nothing happened."

"That might have been the problem. We'll know better when we get the post mortem." Judy drove past the Mitchell's house, and towards the boating lake, along the tree-lined road to where Lloyd lived, in a flat that she had so far resisted visiting. Lloyd felt that tonight was not the night to try again.

"Suppose he did know her?" Judy said, pursuing her theory. "That could be why she didn't want him to give her a lift—why she didn't want to stay in the first place. She did know him, and she wasn't supposed to—two-timing Donald?"

"I've thought of that," he sighed. "However unlikely, I've thought of it. But if that was the case, and he just wanted her dead for some reason, why go to the trouble of making it look like some nut had killed her, and then run away? Surely he'd just have gone home, or back to his sister's, said she'd walked, or—" he broke off. "What am I doing? I don't discuss work when I'm finished for the day. Did Michael get off all right, then?"

"Oh yes," she said, with an edge to her voice. "Michael got off all right. Doesn't he always?"

Lloyd wondered, not for the first time, why she had married Michael, whom at best she merely tolerated. He had known Judy a long time, and he knew when she married that it wasn't likely to work. But you didn't say that to people— you just said you hoped they would be very happy. And he had hoped she would—if she had been, he wouldn't be making even the gentle overtures that he was now. Would he? He liked to think that he wouldn't.

Lloyd had started out in Stansfield, and had met Judy when he moved to London. There, they had worked together until she married, and moved with Michael to Nottingham. He didn't know whose idea it was to come to Stansfield, but he was glad they had. His divorce had forced him to acknowledge the fact that he was lonely, and the subsequent gap in his life had been filled by the re-arrival of Judy. At least it gave him something to think about.

Neat houses, arranged in carefully calculated multi-aspect groups flashed past as Judy exceeded the speed limit with a fine disregard for the law she was sworn to enforce. A drunk made his way unsteadily along the pavement; he was doing no one any harm, and they ignored him. The wind hit the car side-on as they turned into Bunyan Road, creating a draught in the old car that ruffled its passengers' hair.

"If you pull up where that van is," Lloyd said, "that'll be fine. I can nip through the alley." The alley led to the back door of the flats, running through the garages, which were hidden from the road by an ornamental wall.

Judy drew the car smoothly to a halt. "Shall I pick you up in the morning?" she asked.

He opened the door, admitting a blast of air that almost took his breath away. "Please," he said, remembering to close the door in the approved fashion, and waving as she drove away.

Inside, he poured himself a large whisky and sat down in the reclining chair which he had bought himself as a divorce present. His book lay on the table beside it; he picked it up, found his place, and tried to read it. It usually worked, this cutting himself off. No matter how long a day he'd put in, how tired he was, a nightcap and a chapter or two made him feel better. But tonight his thoughts kept returning to Wade and Julia Mitchell and what had gone on at the boating lake.

It was no locked-room mystery, he told himself. The body was not lying on the library floor, stabbed with a jewelled paper knife. There was no figure lurking in the gazebo. Wade had taken the girl up there, and for whatever reason, he had strangled her. He had driven away, gone to his garage in the middle of the night, consumed half a bottle of Scotch—the other half was still there. Then he had fled from justice.

Except, of course, that he hadn't taken her up there. She owned the place—she had the key. It was in her handbag, which they'd found in the café. So she had taken him up there.

He opened his book again. Now he knew what had been nagging at him, he began to relax. Tomorrow he could look for the answer. Outside the wind rattled the windows and howled through the alley, but he felt as he had as a child, when he would play in the outhouse, and the concentrated heat would surround his brown summer body like water. If it rained, streaking the dusty window, it was outside. It couldn't get him.

The wind, moaning and sighing, was outside. It couldn't get him.

The wind carried the sound of the church clock chiming midnight into the Mitchells' house. Helen switched off the bathroom light, and went into the bedroom, where Donald was already in bed, leafing through a magazine. As she sat on the bed to remove her slippers, she could feel the waves of potential serious discussion coming from his side.

"Helen?"

"Yes, Donald." She swung her legs under the bedclothes.

"I've been thinking—about this money." He half turned to face her. "Well, most of it won't be money, of course, it'll be shares in the business. But it's the same thing."

"What about it?" Helen was in no mood for the discussion, but it was impossible to divert Donald once he'd made up his mind.

"You do realise how much we're talking about? Charles was a millionaire—when the radio said he'd made two fortunes, they weren't joking."

"I know, Donald," Helen said impatiently. Charles, in the way of most millionaires, had not been all that open-handed when he was alive, but he had left the boys a great deal of money, not to mention Donald. And now that Donald was getting the rest, she knew what sort of money they were talking about. "Donald—could you get to the point? It's been a very long day."

71

And Donald, she knew, had every intention of making it even longer.

"Well," he said. "I've been thinking—we're not going to carry on living in a semi-detached in Stansfield, are we?"

"No?" she said, stiffening slightly. This just wasn't the time. Her future was not something which particularly concerned her at the moment.

"Oh, don't misunderstand," he said. "I'm not sitting here counting the profits. But there isn't much point in pretending that we've got anything to preserve, is there? And I didn't want you to think that I'd just swan off somewhere once I could." He paused, apparently waiting for her to say something.

Helen couldn't think of anything much to say.

"I will leave," he said. "Whenever we think it's best. But you'll get half of whatever it is I've got by then—I'm not waiting for some judge to sort it out. I just thought you ought to know."

She nodded. "Thank you."

"We could see it coming," he said. "It's just that the money made our minds up. There wouldn't be much point in sticking together so we could be miserable in mink, would there?"

"No." The money had made Donald's mind up. But he was right, of course. "Was it the money?" she asked. "Or had you decided anyway?"

There was a heartbeat before Donald answered. "I'd decided," he said. "When I realised what Chris meant to you."

Helen lay awake in the darkness for a long time, her mind on Chris, as the gales swept in. He must have found somewhere to go, she thought, to comfort herself, but she shivered. So Donald had known all the time—it wasn't too difficult, she supposed. Of all the people in the world, he ought to know the signs.

Judy Hill slept, dreaming that everyone she ever knew was playing tennis in the rain. Her husband wasn't playing; he was standing a little way off, and it wasn't raining where he was. He was complaining, all the same. There was a flapping noise, and a bird swooped down, catching her in its talons. She tried to fight it, but it flapped furiously.

She woke up, her mouth dry, her body tense. The flapping was in the room, and it hurt to move. She lay still, afraid of the noise, until her mind cleared, and she turned to see the curtains billowing out into the room, opened by the wind. The moon was high and small, and silver-edged streams of cloud raced across the sky. Rain, carried on the wind, hit the window as she rose to close it. For some moments she leant on the window sill, looking out at the curve of the road, at the new trees, whose leaves were falling fast. The trees bent in the wind; she wondered if they would survive the wild night.

She lived in the more established part of Stansfield, which meant that the houses were twenty-five years old, and built in terraces, with a single aspect. It also meant that you could not find your way from one end of the street to the other. She had gone down in the folklore of Stansfield Constabulary by having to get a member of the public to get her out again when she had entered one of the new pedestrian estates without a compass. The next day, she had found a distress flare on the passenger seat of the car. She smiled to herself, closed the curtains and went back to bed. She liked Stansfield.

Michael, of course, didn't. But then Michael didn't like anywhere much, and wouldn't, until he could afford to live uptown. Mr. Thingy's Spanish hacienda would suit him down to the ground. Living in a council house was something Michael had never gotten used to, despite having done so from birth. The New York trip meant a lot to him; she wished, a little guiltily, that she had been more enthusiastic for his sake. But then, she argued with herself, everything he does is for his sake, so perhaps he didn't need her blessing. She missed him, in an odd way, when he was off selling computers—this time, he'd only been home two days, and they had been spent sniping at one another, largely because he had failed to sell any computers. And he was worried about

73

New York, because the firm had had to scrape together the money to send him; he desperately wanted to do well.

It was so much easier to be charitable about him when he wasn't there. This morning's row had been the same as all the others—she couldn't remember what had started it, but as always, it ended up being about their standard of living, which suited her and didn't suit Michael. No one in their right minds would live in a place like this, and so on.

And now, of all things, there had been a murder. That was something that Michael would regard as a personal insult if ever there was one. Stansfield had been his idea; she had opened her mouth to tell him that she knew someone there, and had closed it again. Not because it would have put him off, and not because he was likely to read anything into it. Whatever else he was, Michael was not the jealous type. No, she hadn't told him because she knew there was more to it than that. She doubted if she would ever have married Michael if it hadn't been for Lloyd, complete with wife and children.

Perhaps that was what it was with Julia Mitchell. Perhaps they should dig around in her past a little bit, see if Wade figured in it at all. They didn't have to prove motive, but it was so much easier if you knew why someone had done something. She'd look into that tomorrow.

At least he'd got out in time. Chris gulped in the cold air, trying to take all his weight on one foot, then washed in the rainwater that had gathered in the dented roof. Once he was certain he wasn't going to be sick again, he went back inside, shivering and exhausted. But the smell of the store of apples hit him, and he had to go back out. He was sweating, and cold. He thought he might die here, and they would find another body in the woods.

He sat on the step, holding his pounding head, trembling in the wind. No, he wasn't going to die. His system had just rebelled against the whisky and the apples and the pain and the fear. With a great effort of will, he held his breath, and

74

moved his provisions out, throwing them as far away as he could.

He'd had more than enough of being a fugitive. He wasn't even sure why he was one, so tomorrow they could have him. He could keep Helen out of it.

Donald was beginning to feel pleasantly drowsy at last. He had almost forgotten what sleep was like, but now he could feel it stealing up to the edges of his mind, gradually blurring the thought processes. Helen slept beside him, breathing deeply; he wished, in a way, that their marriage could continue. Donald wasn't sure what love was—he didn't think he'd ever loved anyone—but Helen had probably produced an emotion more akin to love than anyone else, and he had no desire to hurt her. But he had done, over and over again, and so in the end she had turned to someone else. That was, as he'd told her, when he knew he must call it a day. If Chris could make her happy, then he mustn't hang about to make her feel guilty.

But now, of course, all this had happened, and who knew what was going to happen next? The whole senseless business was threatening everyone's security, not least Helen's.

But he could make her financially secure, which might in some measure make up for the harm he'd done. It was, he concluded sleepily, the best he could do.

As the storm grew outside, Donald turned in the warmth of his bed, and went to sleep.

The night winds were sweeping the south-east, lashing the sea into a fury, crashing the waves on to the promenades; further inland, trees fell, blocking roads and railway lines. Hen-houses were left roofless, and cold-frames smashed as slates were dislodged.

In Stansfield, garden gates swung squeakily and Coke tins rattled along the town centre streets. Rubbish swirled into the corners in the back-street delivery areas, whipped up from the communal waste bins.

In Thorpe Woods, the wind moaned through the trees,

and the night was alive with the sound of shifting leaves. A hedgehog, seeking shelter, crept under the tangle of nettles and weeds and sniffed curiously at the metal surface. It tempered the wind, and he stayed there.

Inside, Chris Wade tossed and turned on the hard bench, which was not made to accommodate six feet of aching muscle. On the same principle as the hedgehog, he too stayed there.

CHAPTER SIX

LLOYD GOT INTO THE CAR BESIDE HER, HIS MOOD matching the bright Autumn morning. "The cop-shop, driver," he said.

Judy didn't reply. Her interrupted night had made her less than sociable, and she could have done without Lloyd's bonhomie.

"Beautiful day," he said, rolling down the window, and breathing in extravagantly. "Doesn't that do your soul good?"

"No," she said.

"Weather forecast said it would rain later—pity." He grinned. "It would do your soul good, if you'd got one."

"I'm sure it would."

A train rattled past, underneath them, as she drove on to Thorpe Wood Road. The odd one stopped at the station, but most of them roared through, like that one.

"Can you hear the trains at night?" she asked.

"Sometimes, if the wind's in the right direction." He laughed. "Last night you could only hear the wind."

Lloyd lived in old Stansfield, the village that had been there long before the cuckoo in the nest. The flat in which he lived was in one of two blocks, carefully designed to blend in with the atmosphere of the village, as it was still called. The experiment had worked; they were just part of the scenery.

"Oh, look—there's a young tree down," he said. "It's hardly a tree at all—only about an inch thick."

"I thought the one outside our house might fall, but it didn't."

" 'The gale, it plies the sapling double, and thick on Severn snow the leaves,' " Lloyd said, winding up the window as the soul-improving freshness proved too much. "Michael wasn't home very long this time, was he? Had to love you and leave you, did he?"

"In a manner of speaking." She heard herself give an audible, unintentional, sigh.

"It goes on, you know."

She frowned. "What does?"

" 'On Wenlock Edge'—you should listen to it. 'There, like the wind through woods in riot . . .' "

But she didn't listen. She drove, letting the words wash over her. He didn't need a rapt audience—he just needed someone there so that he wasn't too obviously speaking for his own pleasure. She could imagine him as a fiery Welsh minister, threatening cringing congregations with hellfire, pronounced with about five Ls. Dropping his voice for dramatic effect, raising it at precisely the right moment to make them jump. It was a good voice—an actor's voice. It could be full of reassurance, coaxing a story from a frightened child, or cold and unemotional, if he wanted to alarm. He used speech to make up for the fact that he was the only Welshman in the world who couldn't sing.

The carefully controlled Welsh accent broke through her own private thoughts.

" '. . . Today, the Roman and his trouble are ashes under Uricon.' " He paused. "What's wrong?"

"You mean apart from the fact that you're reciting poetry at half past eight in the morning?"

"Poets know a thing or two," he said mildly, "about feelings. More than computer salesmen."

"It wouldn't be hard," she said. "What's put you in such good humour, anyway? You're not usually this cheerful first thing."

"I don't really know. Except that it occurred to me last night that if Wade was in the café with her, she must have taken him there, because she had the key."

Judy thought for a moment. "Why, do you think?"

"Why did she take him in there? God knows, but at least we can try to find out."

"No—why did she have the key?"

"It was her café."

"Yes, but she hardly went around clutching the key to it. She was coming to see it—Donald Mitchell must have had the key in the first place. So why did he give it to her?"

Lloyd shook his head. "We can ask him today—we're going there. I'm going to take Elaine Short up on her suggestion, and find out what Helen Mitchell was doing."

Judy aired her own suggestion about taking a look at Julia's history.

"Do you think Wade might have had an old score to settle?" Lloyd asked. "It's possible, I suppose. But nobody seems to think they recognised one another. Still—that's another thing we can do. See? Things are looking up already."

They crossed the car park as the sun dipped behind a cloud, and the forecast rain began to fall.

"Sir? I've left the reports on your desk—they're both there."

Lloyd smiled broadly. "Today is going to be good," he said to Judy as they collected good mornings and messages walking through the CID room. He pushed open the door and stood flamboyantly aside to let her through.

Judy watched as he scanned the reports. He threw them across to her. "All we have to do is find him," he said.

Judy stooped to retrieve the folder which had, of course, missed her desk and scattered its contents on the floor.

"Sorry," he said.

Julia Mitchell had died between 7:30 P.M. and 9:00 P.M. Death was due to asphyxiation, caused by the restriction of her breathing with tights or a nylon stocking or similar being tightened round her throat. There were minor abrasions, but nothing to suggest that her attacker would be injured in any way. The most noticeable of her injuries was a deep graze below the left eye, in which traces of wood varnish were found. This was thought to have been caused as she lost consciousness and fell, as the small amount of bleeding suggested that it had happened very shortly before death. The blood on the table matched that of the deceased, and the varnish was of a type and age similar to that found in the wound. There was no evidence of sexual activity.

She moved on to the list of stomach contents, listening with half an ear as Lloyd picked up the phone.

"Could you get me Mr. Donald Mitchell, please? His number is Stansfield 3074."

The forensic reports next. They confirmed that she had been in the café; prints matching those found on the steering wheel of Wade's car, on the whisky bottle taken from the garage, and on the shaving mirror taken from Wade's house were found in the café in a number of places, including the door into the boatshed, the counter, and the front door. A jacket which had been identified as Wade's was also found in the café. From the position of the prints on the table, it seemed that he had picked it up and righted it after it had fallen. Another set of prints had yet to be identified; Mr. Donald Mitchell would be asked to give a set of prints for elimination purposes. Several prints were found in the boatshed, which had been operational that day, but no clear prints matching any found in the café. Fibres matching those of the deceased's jacket had been found in Wade's car, and a set of unidentified prints on the dashboard. The deceased's prints were not found in the car.

Judy looked up. "Did you read that bit?" she asked, as Lloyd put the phone down. "About her prints not being found in Wade's car?"

"Yes—but I don't think it means much, really. If he's a door opener, for instance. Opens the door—all she has to do is get in. Opens the door for her to leave—and she gets out. She wouldn't have to touch anything that would leave any prints."

Judy pursed her lips. "What about the other prints, though?"

"We'll have to see what Wade says about them. Might be his sister's, for all we know. We can check that, unless he enlightens us first."

"You don't think he could have gone up there with someone else altogether?" Judy found herself hoping that he had, and didn't know why.

"I hope not," Lloyd said, smiling, "or we'd better start looking for another body—he came back without her, remember."

"And he's disappeared," Judy said, resignedly. "I think he must have gone up there with her."

"Don't sound so wistful. You haven't even met him and you're beginning to sound like his sister. Chris didn't do it."

Judy looked at him. "Tell me honestly," she said. "Are you convinced that he did?"

"She was dead by nine o'clock—right? He took her up there at half past eight. Or at the very least, he left the Shorts' house with her at twenty past, and was at the café by half past. What else is there to think?"

"He could have dropped her off there, and gone home."

"Stopping only to leave his jacket and his prints? And anyway, she was dead by the time he left—these people leave a margin for error—you know that."

Judy accepted that her theory didn't really hold water.

"I've just asked Mitchell to come in," he said. "To establish that the other set of prints in the café are his. If they are—" he shrugged. "Like I said, all we have to do is find Wade."

Donald went into the kitchen, where Helen was washing up.

"They want me to go in," he said. "To have my fingerprints taken."

Helen turned round. "Why?"

"Elimination, he says. So that they can sort out what's what at the café." He poured himself some more tea. "Do you want another cup? It's still hot."

"No, thank you. Did he say anything else?"

"Not really. Just that they would be destroyed immediately." He laughed. "In case I commit a crime some time in the future. It wouldn't be playing the game, you see, if they already had my fingerprints." He stirred his tea. "And they want to clear up a couple of things about Julia, apparently. So I'll pop up there, and then I'll go straight for my train—unless you want me here for any reason?"

"I don't think so." Helen looked pale and drawn.

"He says someone will be coming here some time this morning to have another word with you—but you won't need me for that, will you?"

Helen agreed that she wouldn't, and Donald went to get ready.

He wondered what they wanted to know about Julia. Probably something he couldn't tell them. They seemed to think he knew her every move. Including, he remembered, her father's hotel in Spain. He had decided to tell them about the will—it wouldn't really do for them to find out from someone else. It might look a bit odd.

"I'm going to tell them about the money," he said to Helen as she passed him in the hall. He shrugged on his raincoat. "I think I'd better, don't you?"

"What's it got to do with them?" Helen asked, with an automatic privacy preserving reaction.

"Nothing. But I think I'd better—just so they know all the facts. You don't mind, do you?"

Helen made a shrugging gesture, and he assumed that she didn't mind.

Chris opened his eyes, which met the rusting walls. He blinked for a moment, then tried to move, but every muscle ached from the exertions of the night. He sat up slowly, light-headed and sore. His ankle throbbed painfully as he tried to stand, and he fell back on to the bench, his back against the moist wall. The swimming sensation left him at last, as he opened his eyes again. At least he didn't feel sick any more. He felt exhausted, and frightened, but he didn't feel sick. He

82

took a deep breath, and launched himself out into the open, stumbling round, searching for something that would serve as a walking stick. Hopping from tree to tree, his hands clutching the wet bark, he scanned the ground until at last he saw a thin branch long enough and strong enough to support him.

The rain was falling in a steady drizzle as he made rather quicker progress through the trees back to his den. He couldn't make it up to the town. He'd wait there until he saw a policeman. He was bound to see one sooner or later.

"Did they come here at all to your knowledge, Mrs. Mitchell?"

Helen wasn't sure how good she was going to be at lying to this efficient young woman with the frank brown eyes.

"No—but they could have. I wasn't here all the time."

"Oh?" Sergeant Hill seemed to be showing nothing more than polite interest.

They were in the sitting room, and the sergeant sat where Chris had. Helen looked out at the garden, which sloped gently towards the pine wood, and she wondered where he was, hiding in its denseness. She wished she was out there, walking through its green solitude, dreaming of life as it should be.

Life as it was sat opposite her, pen in hand, notebook on the coffee table, smart and cool and organised. Her life, Helen felt sure, wouldn't dare to have messy edges.

"Yes. I had to take a friend to the station. She decided to get the earlier train—the 8:50. We left just after Donald phoned for Julia. About half past, I suppose. Perhaps a little later."

"Do you know why your husband wanted to speak to Julia?"

Helen picked up her cigarettes. "They'd had an argument—he wanted to apologise, I believe." She felt guilty even when she was telling the truth. She lit a cigarette, and waited for the next question. The sergeant was writing it all

83

down, and she was talking too much. Don't volunteer information, she told herself. Let her ask.

"Could I have your friend's name and address, please?"

"Is that really necessary? I'd much rather she wasn't dragged into this—"

"I'm afraid so, Mrs. Mitchell. We have to check."

"Why?"

"Because all that we know for a fact is that your sister-in-law is dead, and that Mr. Wade is missing. We don't know if he's still alive—so we have to know what everyone was doing at the material time."

Helen reluctantly agreed that that seemed reasonable. Poor Margaret—she only came for the day, and now she was going to get policemen demanding to know her movements. Margaret was an old school friend, with whom Helen had kept up for the thirty-five years that had passed since their hockey-playing days. She wished she were here now, so down to earth and sensible—she'd know how to deal with this. She wouldn't feel afraid of a young woman with a notebook and pencil.

Helen told the sergeant Margaret's name and address, with a heavy heart. Her opinion of Julia hadn't exactly been glowing, either, she remembered, with a smile. As soon as she had established that Julia and Helen weren't bosom friends, they had had a lovely gossip about her. She stubbed out her cigarette.

"So—you ran your friend to the station, and she caught her train. What time did you get back?"

"About half past nine," Helen said. "Maybe twenty-five to ten."

The sergeant looked up then, with an enquiring look.

Don't volunteer, Helen told herself again. Let her ask. Let her *ask*.

"It was Stansfield station?" she asked, pleasantly enough.

"Yes."

Was it her imagination, or was Sergeant Hill allowing irritation to cross her composed features?

"And what time did you leave the station?" Still the rou-

84

tine pleasantness. No bare light bulbs, no rubber hoses. Just an attractive young woman, in Helen's own dining room, wearing a cool, pastel-striped shirt that in other circumstances Helen would have asked her about.

"I'm not sure—I stayed there a few moments. A couple of minutes to nine, I imagine."

"So you didn't come straight home?"

"Yes." She had to enlarge on that. "I did, but the storm broke as I came into Thorpe Wood Road, and I couldn't see a thing. I waited in the lay-by until the rain had eased up."

"I see." She smiled at Helen. "So you were at the lay-by at about—what—five past nine, or so? Possibly earlier?"

"I must have been."

"Did you see Mr. Wade's car—or any car, for that matter?"

Helen's heart was beating so loudly that she was sure it could be heard outside the room. Her throat muscles tightened. How much of the truth?

"No," she said, trying to sound natural, and failing. She twisted her ring round and round. When was she going to stop asking questions?

"Why didn't you mention this to the inspector yesterday?" she was asking.

"I didn't think. I'm sorry."

"But we were asking for anyone who was in the area— you did realise that you might be a witness?"

"No—the radio said anyone who had seen them. I didn't see them."

The sergeant seemed to accept this, and moved on.

"You got back to the house at about half past nine or so— I believe your husband had been trying to contact you?"

How did they know that, for crying out loud? "Yes," she said grudgingly.

"Why?"

It's none of your business, Helen thought. Aloud, she said: "To tell me he was waiting for the storm to ease off, and he'd be later than he thought."

"Did you discuss Mrs. Mitchell?"

"No. Well—yes, he asked if she was there, and I said not yet, or something."

Sergeant Hill wrote something in her notebook, and Helen stood up, stiff with tension. "Would you like a cup of tea, Sergeant Hill?"

"No thank you, Mrs. Mitchell. I don't want to keep you any longer than necessary."

Helen cast an almost furtive glance at the clock. Nearly eleven o'clock. She'd been here for three-quarters of an hour.

"Soon be finished," Sergeant Hill said cheerfully, as though she'd read her mind.

It was almost over then. Helen sat down again quickly, feeling giddy with relief.

"I'd just like you to think back to when you came back from the station," she said evenly, as though the subject hadn't come up before. "Did you see any cars on the way back?"

Helen didn't answer, as she tried desperately to think of something to say.

"Mrs. Mitchell?" There was a no-nonsense air about her now, like a nanny.

"Of course there were cars," she said testily. "Am I supposed to remember them all?"

"What ones do you remember?" She spoke in the same, even tones.

"What difference does it make?" Helen jumped up, and took another cigarette out of the packet. "You've made your mind up, anyway. You've given his description on the radio—you're talking about using dogs!"

The sergeant also stood, and offered her a cigarette lighter.

Helen waved it away, half turning so that she was not facing her inquisitor.

"We want to talk to him," she said. "And either something's happened to him too, or he's hiding from us. Whichever—we do have to look for him." She sat down again, composed and collected, and looked up at Helen. "Did you see Mr. Wade's car on Saturday night?"

Helen found a box of matches, and shook it, only to find

86

that it was empty. With an exclamation of annoyance, she threw it down on to the table, where it bounced off and fell to the ground.

Coolly, as ever, Sergeant Hill took out the lighter again, suggesting with her eyes that Helen sit down. Despite being irritated almost beyond endurance, Helen complied, and Sergeant Hill flicked the lighter, which lit first time. Helen knew that if the roles had been reversed, her lighter would have clicked impotently and destroyed the whole effect. The flame burned steadily, and her need for a cigarette overcame her desire to leave her sitting there like the Statue of Liberty.

"Did you see Mr. Wade's car?"

Helen inhaled deeply, and expelled blue-grey smoke into the fresh, sunlit room. It hung almost motionless in the shaft of light from the window, and it was through the haze of smoke and sun that she looked defiantly at the sergeant, a small muscle working at the side of her face. She had been lulled into a false sense of security, and she resented it.

"There were cars," she said. "Other cars."

"Tell me about them." She held her pen at the ready over her notebook.

"I don't know—there was a motorbike just beyond the lay-by as I drew in. They were stopped just by the pathway to the boating lake."

"They?"

"Two people—a boy and a girl." Helen smoked quickly in between sentences. "And another car—I don't know what kind. It was open, in all that rain, and the driver was getting soaked." She was talking quickly now—too quickly, the words tumbling out. "That was while I had the windscreen wipers going, but then I switched them off and I didn't see anything else. I wasn't taking particular—" she stopped, perilously close to tears. "Why couldn't it have been one of them? Why does it have to be Chris?" She turned her head away to try to hide the tears.

"It doesn't have to be," the sergeant said. "That's why I'm asking you what you saw."

87

Liar, thought Helen, looking back at her as a kind of control asserted itself.

"What colour was the car with the open top?"

"Dark—I'm not sure what colour. It was dark." Smoke came with the words. "I mean—it was night time, and the car was dark."

"Did you see Mr. Wade's car?" Still exactly the same tone of voice, as though it was the first time she'd asked.

"No."

"I know Mr. Wade is a friend of yours," she said.

Helen drew herself up. She would have no criticism of their friendship, not from her or anyone else. "We've made no secret of it," she said. "My husband told your Inspector."

"You might think you're helping him, but you're not—believe me, you're not."

"I don't know what you mean." Smoke curled up from the cigarette between her fingers, and twisted into thinning strands.

"We have witnesses, Mrs. Mitchell. Witnesses who saw Mr. Wade's car leave the boating lake at nine o'clock, and turn right towards the village. Towards his garage, we presume, since he was seen there later. Towards the station, come to that. Did you see his car?"

It was her house. She could just walk out of the room. She could tell Sergeant Hill to leave—she had the right. "I don't have to answer you," she said.

"But you do. You know you do. You can't withhold information, Mrs. Mitchell. I don't think I have to tell you that."

Helen made a small, defeated noise. "All right. Yes, I saw his car. Does that satisfy you?"

"When did you see it?" Her expression hadn't changed. No triumph.

"Just before it rained. He passed me. That doesn't mean he killed her."

"Did he see you?"

"I don't know. It was at the mini-roundabout where Wood Thorpe Road and Main Street join—he was waiting for a car.

88

I could see him, but I don't think he saw me." She thought for a moment, then realised that her statement was misleading. "I don't mean I could see him—I could see the car. I didn't see who was inside it, so I assumed Julia was with him." She saw the look on the sergeant's face. "I'm not just saying that," she said. "I just saw the car. It was at the opposite side of the road, on the other side of the roundabout, and there was a car going round between us. When Donald rang, I said Chris must have found no one in and taken her back to his house—I just assumed she was with him."

The sergeant wrote all this down with what seemed to Helen like exaggerated care.

"I'm sorry," Helen said. "I should have told you in the first place. I just didn't know what to do."

"We do understand, Mrs. Mitchell."

"We!" Helen put as much contempt into the single syllable as she could. "Why do you people always call yourselves 'we'?"

"All right—*I* understand, then."

Helen shook her head.

"Sir?"

Lloyd looked up, and then up again. "Yes, Constable Sandwell."

"I was just thinking—do you remember when they built that road?"

"Which road would that be?" Lloyd stood up to mark off on the map the latest part of the wood to be searched. Turning to face Sandwell, he decided to sit down again, to minimise the inadequacy of his height.

"Thorpe Wood Road. They built it alongside the wood, and then they planted the pine trees. It would be about ten years ago."

"No. I'd left Stansfield then—I was in the big city. What about it?"

"Well, sir," Sandwell began. "I was about nine or ten then."

Lloyd groaned.

89

"Sorry, sir." Sandwell smiled. "But when they'd finished, there was one of these workmen's huts left on site. And there were arguments about which of the contractors had used it, and which should move it and so on—and me and my mates used to play in it. Nobody would do anything about it—and we used it for ages. When they began planting the new trees—to extend the pine wood, they shifted it back from the road, and eventually you couldn't see it at all. I don't think anyone ever moved it."

Lloyd smiled broadly at Sandwell. "When did this thought hit you?" he asked.

"Just now sir. I was saying to Sergeant Watson about how the town had changed, and I just remembered. Do you think he could be there?"

Judy walked in.

"Don't take your coat off, Sergeant, you're not stopping." Lloyd stood up. "Come on, Sherlock—get weaving. You can drive us there—if you're right, the arrest's down to you. You'll get your name in the papers."

Sandwell, delighted, went off to get the car, and Lloyd explained to Judy, who was looking slightly startled at the sudden burst of action.

"So," Lloyd said. "Perhaps we can wrap it up now."

Judy didn't look so sure. "Perhaps," she said. "But I've a feeling we don't know the half of it yet."

Lloyd hesitated, then laughed at himself. "He'll just give up," he said. "You'll see. He'll tell us the lot."

The bird that was lying in wait for a rash worm to be drawn to the surface by the intermittent rain flew off as the car drew up. From the safety of a tree, he watched the group of people cross the muddy grass towards the pine wood.

Another figure appeared, bearded and limping, walking towards the group with the aid of a stick. He tried to run, but he couldn't, and he stumbled as he did so. One of the other people helped him, and they took him to the car.

With difficulty, they put him in the back, and then they all got back in again, and drove off. Once they had turned in the road, and were on their way back where they came from, the bird flew down again, and continued his wait for a worm.

If he was very patient, one would turn up sooner or later, like buses.

Like policemen.

CHAPTER SEVEN

JUDY FINISHED EATING, AND LOOKED REFLEC-tively at Lloyd, then at the room. "You look after yourself all right, don't you?"

"What did you expect?" He laughed. "Beer cans on the bare floorboards?"

"No—just less comfort."

Lloyd looked round at the shabby old furniture, shown up even more by the reclining chair in which Judy was doing just that. "I got all this lot from a second hand shop," he said. "You've got the only comfortable chair there is."

She smiled. "But it looks so nice—it reminds me of when I was small. It's the sort of furniture my mum had."

"It probably is your mum's."

She laughed, and stretched luxuriously. "I could fall asleep," she said. "You'd better engage me in sparkling conversation."

"Do you think Helen Mitchell's told you everything now?"

"I don't know," Judy said drowsily, and sat up. "I really am falling asleep. She could have, but I feel as though she's still holding something back." She yawned.

"Why do I feel as though everyone's lying to us?" Lloyd got up to make coffee.

"Automatic reaction," Judy said, as he went off to the kitchen. "We're the fuzz."

"The enemy?" Lloyd said, raising his voice. "Not usually of sober, white collar, middle-income bracket citizens, we're not. Unless we've got them on a motoring offence."

He didn't hear what she said, as he ground up the coffee. When the coffee maker was going about its business, he went back in, to find Judy lighting a cigarette.

"I thought you'd given up?"

"I still smoke occasionally," she said.

"And this is an occasion?" He sat down, then thought he'd better clear away the debris of the Chinese meal that they had eaten picnic style out of the tinfoil containers.

"Well, it's the first time I've seen your flat," she said, piling things up for him. "That makes it an occasion."

It certainly did for him, he thought, as he tipped his load into the swingbin.

"Who else do you think is lying?" she asked, suddenly at his elbow.

"I spoke to Mitchell about the key—he says she asked for it, and he gave it to her. He had no idea why." He got mugs out of the cupboard. "I suppose he did. But I got the feeling that the question—" he searched for the word. "Discommoded him," he said.

"Do you think they're covering up for Wade—they know something damaging that they're not telling us?"

"Could be." Lloyd poured the coffee, and handed Judy hers. They would insist on sending Wade to hospital for a check-up. He was beginning to think that the doctor did it on purpose to give the patients time to think up a good story. "I'll be glad when I can talk to Wade himself."

They carried their coffee back through to the living room.

"Do you want the comfortable chair?" Judy asked.

"No, no. You're the guest—you have it." He sat down again on the unyielding sofa. "You're having a go at Mrs. Short after lunch?"

"Yes," she said. "When you're becoming a star of the silver screen."

"It wasn't my idea—it was Randall. 'You're better at that sort of thing, Inspector.' How does he know? I've never been on television."

93

Judy grinned. "Only because of some grave oversight. Could it be he thinks you like the sound of your own voice? Surely not."

"Shut up."

They finished their coffee, and got up to go. Lloyd picked up Judy's coat and held it for her.

"Thank you," she said, slipping her arm in. "By the way, I took a phone call for you this morning while you were with Mitchell." She turned to face him. "They wanted to know why you hadn't picked your car up on Friday as arranged." She smiled sweetly. "So do I."

Lloyd thought fast, but no plausible excuse presented itself. The truth, then. "You know why," he said.

"So that I'd chauffeur you around."

"It's not a chauffeur I'm looking for." He could have phrased it better, but it didn't seem to matter. "Why didn't you tell me before lunch?"

"Same reason," she said. "But I'm not sure it's a very good reason."

Lloyd took her hands in his. "You once said you couldn't have anything to do with me because I was married."

"So I did." She smiled.

"I'm not married now."

"I am." But it was just a statement of fact, not a protest. She took a step towards him, and her lips touched his as the phone rang. She stepped back, leaving the way clear to the phone.

"Thank you very much," Lloyd said to it, and picked it up.

"Rogers here, sir. They've found her underwear—bra, pants and tights."

"Great. Where?"

"A long way from either the body or the rest of her clothes, I'm told. The lab's got them now. Can we call off the search?"

"Er—yes. Yes. I think so. But keep the area roped off—and have someone keeping an eye on it. I don't want sightseers."

"Right, sir."

Lloyd replaced the receiver and relayed the call to Judy.

"Well," she said, good humouredly. "Is that the end of the seduction scene?"

Lloyd laughed, and opened the front door. Lunch, a laugh, and a stillborn kiss. It was better than nothing.

They were in Charles Mitchell's tasteful drawing room, not speaking much. Donald had something to say, but he had not yet fully worked out how he was going to say it.

Maria smiled; he just smiled back, like a stranger, like someone in a waiting room. He touched her to prove that he wasn't.

"It takes a bit of getting used to," she said. "That's all."

"I know," he said, taking her hand in his. It was cold—he rubbed it gently. "I can't stay," he said. "I've got to get back."

"You said." She took her hand away and stood up. "I'll get your photograph. It's in the bedroom."

Donald walked round the room, touching the delicate furniture. He ran his hand over the smooth polished wood of the table.

"It's yours now," she said, reappearing at the door. "Isn't it?"

"I think so," he said. "It's a bit complicated, as I said." He took the photograph, and glanced at its general amateur fuzziness. "There aren't any others?" he asked.

"No. Won't that one do?" She came over to him, and looked at it over his shoulder, pushing the fair hair away from her face.

"It'll have to, I suppose." He gave her a proprietorial peck on the cheek, and put the photograph down. "Are you going to be all right?"

"Don't worry about me, Donald," she said, with a touch of sarcasm. "You've got more than enough on your plate."

He'd have to tell her. Donald crossed his fingers for luck—not, for once, because he was lying. "I've told Helen," he said.

"About me?" she asked sharply.

"No, of course not. I told you—it's a point of honour. But I have told her I'm leaving. I can't just now, not with all this. But I've told her I will be going."

"Well, well. And I thought now you'd got all this money, you'd just pension me off." She smiled.

He could have, of course. But Maria had lasted longer than anyone, and he hadn't outgrown her yet. They were holding each other, and the waiting room atmosphere had gone. Maria had been waiting for the blow to fall, and it hadn't. But Donald's fingers were still crossed. "There is one thing," he said. "I've told her she'll have half the money."

"Half the money from the will?" She looked horrified.

"Yes. Don't worry—it leaves more than enough for anyone. How much do you suppose this place is worth, for instance?"

"Too much," she said. "But even at that. Aren't you being a little over-generous?"

"I don't think so," he said. "I'd say it was the least I could do. Helen's had a rough deal."

"Oh well, you know me. I wouldn't have known what he was worth—too many noughts for me to understand."

"I could have lied to you," he said. "But I'd rather you knew the position." He put his arms round her. "It was just that I thought she'd have Chris Wade, but God knows what'll happen now. It was the only thing I thought might make up for everything."

"Are you sure you *want* to leave her?" It was a serious question, and she was waiting for an answer.

Donald had never had to face the truth so much in his life, and he found it exhausting. "No, I'm not," he said with an honesty that took her aback. "But I do want you, and she doesn't want me any more. All this money," he said. "It forces you to look at what's happening, and think about the future. You can't just pocket it and get on with your life."

"This friend of yours has done everyone a favour, then," she said.

"I wish to God he hadn't," Donald said.

"There's nothing you can do, Donald."

"No." He looked at his watch. "I have got to go—I'll try to phone you. I probably won't be able to get back for a little while." He looked round. "Where did I put the photograph?"

"On the table. Oh—I got that address. It might not be much good." Maria took a sheet of paper from a drawer. "It's the firm's travel agent—her father might have used them. I can't think of anything else."

"Thanks." He took out his wallet. "You're sure there isn't another photograph?" He put it in his wallet as he spoke.

"Quite sure—at least, I can't find any more. She wasn't keen on having her photograph taken, funnily enough."

"She was probably wanted on three continents," Donald said, and made her laugh for the first time.

She gave him a kiss. "Hurry back," she said.

Donald would be back in about an hour. Helen made herself a cup of tea, and settled down to her hourly ritual of waiting for the news. Now that their marriage was officially over, now that the words had actually been spoken, she could worry as openly as she liked. Donald would be all right; he'd got money enough to satisfy any ambition that had previously been frustrated. She wondered what he would do—go to London, she suspected, to set up in style. He might even live in Charles's house—it was his kind of place. And there would be no shortage in London of a girl or two to keep him company. But, please God, not one like Julia.

If Donald had to stray, why did he have to have such bad taste in women? And why was it so easy for him to have affairs, when she couldn't bring herself to have even one? Chris thought it was because of the age difference, but it wasn't. She was of the old school, and she had promised to keep only unto Donald. Two wrongs didn't make a right. But now that Donald was going, and she might lose Chris, the promise began to seem futile. She regretted and resented her fidelity, if you called it fidelity. Feelings were more important than physical acts, and her feelings were with Chris, and no one else.

The news dealt with what it considered to be the most important matters first, and then the word Stansfield came. *"Stansfield police confirmed this afternoon that the man they wish to interview in connection with the death of thirty-five year old Julia Mitchell on Saturday night has given himself up to the police.*

"No charges have yet been brought, and it is believed that the man is in hospital recovering from an injury."

Relief, despair, fear, worry—Helen didn't know which one to feel first. He was hurt. He was caught, but then he always was going to be. He was safe, and that was the main thing.

Chris had broken a small bone in his foot, he was informed. They would be giving him a crutch, and teaching him how to use it, and then he could be released to the police. In the few moments that he had to wait, he could relax.

The bed was heaven, and he lay back on the pillow, cut off from the rest of the ward by screens, but listening to his fellow patients indulging in verbal slap and tickle with the nurses. At least he was clean and warm and shaved; at least he wasn't hiding any more. Although he was in a ward, he was fully clothed, in the new clothes that Elaine had brought, because the police took away his others. He lay on a bed where they had put him, out of the way. They hadn't let him see Elaine, which was a pity.

But it would be all right. He hadn't killed her, so he had nothing to be afraid of, or so everyone said. He would have liked to have seen Elaine, though, to tell her that he was all right, and that she hadn't got to worry.

They were a long time coming with this crutch. He'd close his eyes. The warmth and comfort claimed him, and he fell sound asleep.

Judy tried to comfort Elaine Short, who paced up and down the room as she spoke.

"He's quite well, Mrs. Short."

She stopped in mid-pace. "He didn't kill her," she said. "He had no reason to!"

"He's not been charged yet. Are you absolutely sure that he didn't know Julia? From some time in the past, perhaps?"

"He didn't know her," she said helplessly. "I can't prove it—I can only tell you. Martin knew her, though."

"Could Chris have met her through your husband?"

"No—Martin had met her at meetings and things, but he didn't know her, not the way you mean. And Chris certainly didn't."

Judy waited until her pacing brought her level. "How can you be so sure? Did you know everyone your brother knew? You lived a long way away from him for years."

The rain coursed down the patio window, obscuring the view, closing everything in. "He'd have said," she explained, with exaggerated patience. "He knew she was coming—he'd have mentioned it."

"Not if he had some reason not to."

"You mean if he was going to murder her?" Elaine threw up her hands in a gesture of frustration. "But you're going round in circles—and he didn't know her."

"But you will accept that it's a possibility?"

"It's a possibility that he knows Glenda Jackson, but I know he doesn't!"

Judy smiled. "All right—you're right, we're going round in circles."

"Why is he in hospital—why is he being kept in, if he's quite all right?"

Judy took a deep breath, this being the third time she had answered that particular question. "Because he has an ankle injury. They'll be releasing him this afternoon. He is honestly all right. There's nothing to worry about."

Elaine stopped pacing. "Oh, no," she said. "Nothing at all. You're just going to say that he murdered someone. That's nothing to worry about—" she held the back of her hand to her mouth, and tried to stop the tears.

Great, thought Judy, that's great. Well done, that's the second one you've reduced to tears today. What a lovely job.

"Please, Mrs. Short. Don't distress yourself—sit down."

"I am not distressing myself! This business is distressing me," she shouted, but she sat down, beside Judy on the sofa.

Judy nodded in what she hoped was an understanding manner. It certainly ought to be, because this business wasn't doing her much good either.

"She came in here," Elaine said, angrily. "She came in here, looking for a fight with someone. Maybe she just picked on Chris, and . . ." She shook her head. "No. No, I don't believe it. He didn't kill her." She blew her nose.

Judy patted her shoulder. "I can't pretend that it looks good for your brother," she said. "But it could have been something like that—if he was provoked, it's possible that they—"

"I don't think she had the least intention of staying," Elaine said suddenly, interrupting Judy and saving her from having to finish the sentence. "She didn't look as though she was staying." She paused for a moment, and considered carefully before she spoke. "Have you ever done any acting?" she asked.

"Acting?" Judy said. "No—"

"Well, I have. You see—I'm sorry, I don't know your name."

"Judy Hill."

"Judy. I used to act—nothing spectacular, and not for very long, but I did, before I met Martin. And you know the old cliché situation in plays when someone is walking to the door, and gets called back at the last minute?"

Judy did.

"Well, if you're acting in a play, you've read the script—you know you're going to get called back. And so, unless you're careful, you *look* as though you know. We'd get told to remember that it was up to the other actor to call us back—we had to believe we were going to walk through the door—do you know what I mean?"

"Yes, I know."

"Julia looked as though she had no intention of staying. She looked as though she was going to leave, long before Donald called her a bitch." She shrugged, and smiled a quick, apologetic smile. "I haven't tried to explain that to anyone else."

Judy said she would bear it in mind. It only strengthened her supposition that Julia knew Chris from somewhere, and had made up her mind to leave the moment she clapped eyes on him, but she didn't voice this opinion to Elaine.

"Until we know what your brother has to say, we don't know what's important and what isn't. That's why we're trying to find out exactly what happened—and what you felt happened," she added.

Elaine smiled. "Will Chris—I mean, he should have a solicitor, shouldn't he?"

Judy stood up. "Yes, I rather think he should," she said. "He hasn't asked for one yet."

"Can he ring me? He's allowed to phone someone, isn't he?"

"Yes." Judy would get him to ring her if it was the last thing he did. "Don't worry, please. We haven't heard his side of it yet."

"He couldn't," Elaine was still assuring her as she made it to the front door. "He just couldn't."

She was glad to get away before she found herself agreeing with Mrs. Short that her brother couldn't possibly kill a fly.

The fly that had indeed remained unmolested by Chris Wade still buzzed around the workmen's hut, and around the policeman who was checking it. He was waved away, and flew out into the afternoon, where the fitful weather was now shining and summer-like.

He flew across the road, to the building with all the people round it. People meant sandwiches, and mayonnaise jar lids, and sugar.

He settled on a camera lens, and was waved away again, towards the boating lake. Ducks—ducks meant bread. He swooped down on a crust that had missed the water.

This was the life.

CHAPTER EIGHT

THE NIGHTMARE WAS CLOSING IN. CHRIS HAD rung Elaine, told her that he didn't want a solicitor. His reasoning was that only guilty people needed solicitors, and he wanted to tell them anything, everything they wanted to know. Elaine had sounded doubtful; he had demanded angrily to know why. Did she believe he'd killed Julia Mitchell? No, of course not, she had said. But perhaps you should get a solicitor.

He sat at a formica-covered table, in a smallish room, the walls of which were bare except for the NOTICE TO PERSONS IN POLICE CUSTODY, which he had read and re-read until he could recite it. They hadn't charged him yet, which must mean something, presumably. The constable who had remained in the room with him stared straight ahead, not speaking. It was hard to believe he was even thinking, or breathing come to that. He was standing at the moment, at the side of the door, so Chris assumed that he wasn't dead. But then, he thought gloomily, he had assumed Julia wasn't dead.

The inspector had asked him for his version of events, and he'd given it, without interruption. There was a moment while the inspector seemed to be mulling it over, and then he had abruptly left the room, stopping only to advise Chris to think about it.

Think about it. Chris almost laughed. Think about it! He'd

thought of nothing else. The steady rain beat down outside, and he tried smiling at the constable, but got no response.

The door opened, and the inspector was back. "Right," he said, sitting opposite him. "Let's hear it again. From the beginning."

Chris sighed. "I gave her a lift home from my sister's house."

"Did you know her? Had you met her before?"

"No." Chris wondered what he was getting at.

"Why did you give her a lift?"

"Do I have to know someone before I offer them a lift? She was leaving, that's all."

Lloyd leant back in his chair. "She'd only just arrived, hadn't she?"

"Yes," Chris said. "She didn't want to stay."

Lloyd nodded, and pushed his chair back so that it squeaked on the tiled floor. He walked to the window. "Did she want a lift?"

"What?"

"You heard."

"She said she was going to walk."

"So? Why were you so keen to give her a lift?" He tutted at the rain, and waited for a reply.

"I wasn't! It was getting dark, and it's a lonely road— there was going to be a storm."

"A lonely road," Lloyd repeated. "It is, isn't it?"

"Yes!"

Lloyd turned quickly. "Did she want a lift? Did she say yes, thank you?"

"No, she—"

"What?"

"She said she'd walk." Chris traced a crack in the formica with his fingernail.

"So what did you do?"

"I said she should let me drive her home."

Lloyd turned back to the window. "Along the lonely road." He leant over and looked out, craning his neck as though he were trying to see something, and wasn't really interested in the conversation at all. "How many times did she refuse?"

Chris stared at the back of his head, and the patch of scalp showing through the dark hair. "I don't know," he said, alarmed.

"I do. Four times, according to your brother-in-law. Three or four times, he said." Lloyd faced him, and smiled. "But you insisted, didn't you?"

"I suppose so—I just thought . . ." Chris tailed off. He had insisted.

"All right—so she got a lift, whether she wanted one or not. Then what?"

"It wasn't like that—I just—"

"I don't care what it was like! Then what?" Lloyd was leaning over him, hands on the table. Chris shrank back.

"We were going along Thorpe Wood Road, and she asked me to stop the car. I pulled up in the lay-by."

"Why did she want you to stop?"

"She said she thought she'd lost her pen—she looked in her bag for it, and said she must have left it in the café."

"Her pen. What made her suddenly realise she'd lost her pen? Writing postcards, was she?"

"I don't know. I've told you all this already."

"And I listened, Mr. Wade. But now my critical faculties have been improved by a cup of tea, and now I want to know why."

"I don't know!" Chris roared, then took a deep breath. "Sorry."

"Quite all right, Mr. Wade. All right, she'd lost her pen. Then what happened?"

"We've been through all this," Chris said. "She looked for it, and decided she must have left it in the café. So I took her up there."

"Ah yes—you took her up there." Lloyd sat down again. "At her request?"

Chris closed his eyes. "No, not really."

"You insisted again, did you?"

"She said I had just to go on. She'd walk from there."

104

Lloyd tilted his chair back and looked at him for a long time, until he began to feel even more uncomfortable than he had.

"I didn't like the idea of her going in there alone—it's in the middle of the wood, practically. So I said I'd take her up there."

"But she didn't want you to?" Lloyd let his chair fall forward with a thud.

"No, I suppose she didn't. Look—I thought last night—she might have wanted to—" It sounded crazy now.

"Yes?"

"To—kill herself. And that could be why she didn't want me to come with her. Could she?" They hadn't told him how she'd died. It was still a hope.

Lloyd stared at him. "I see," he said in tones of extremely Welsh wonderment. "If a girl doesn't want your company it must be because she's suicidal? Oh—I've never been that fortunate. Usually, if a girl doesn't want me it's because she's got something much more interesting to do—that doesn't usually include killing herself."

"Could she?" Chris persisted.

"Let's say it's unlikely, shall we?" Lloyd smiled.

"How did she die?"

"Now, Mr. Wade—you know how she died. But we digress. She got taken up to the café whether she wanted to be taken or not." He stood up again, and stretched. "It's been another long day," he said to Chris. "So, you take her up there—go on."

"When we got to the café, she said she'd just run in and see if her pen was there."

Lloyd leant over the table again. "Who opened the door?"

Chris didn't know what that had got to do with it, but he'd told them he'd tell them everything. "She did—she had the key."

"No—you misunderstand. Who opened the car door?"

"Oh—I see." He didn't really, but it was easy enough. "I did. It's very stiff—so I leant over and opened it for her."

105

"You leant over and opened it for her—you did open it, did you?"

"Yes. Why—"

"An old trick, but a good one, in my book. Leaning over to open the door—gives you the proximity necessary to make further progress."

"It was nothing like that! I'd have to lean over to open it for anyone who wasn't used to it."

"And so she nipped in and got her pen, did she?" Lloyd was walking round now, disconcertingly.

"No."

"No!" He was overdoing the incredulity a bit, Chris thought, beginning to get his measure.

"No. She came back out and said the light wasn't working and it might take a little while, so I should just go on, and she'd get home herself."

"And you said rightie-oh, and went on your way?"

"No."

Lloyd sat down in sheer amazement. "Fancy that. What did you say?"

"I said I had a torch in the car, and I'd come and help her look for it." Chris spoke through his teeth. Every word seemed to make matters worse.

"In the café where the light wasn't working? In the lonely café in the middle of the wood? Did she say oh yes please?"

"No." Chris looked at him. "No, she didn't. But I went in anyway."

"Persistent, aren't you, Mr. Wade? You must have taken quite a shine to her."

Chris shook his head.

"Most of us would have been put off by now. She didn't seem to want your company. There must have been a reason for your persistence."

There was a reason for his persistence. Of course there was.

But it had nothing whatever to do with Julia.

* * *

106

"The boating lake murder—a man is taken in for questioning."

Thus began the ITV news, and Helen watched it with a gin and tonic and a cigarette for company. Donald had come back, and gone straight out again to the police to see if Chris needed his help.

"The man wanted in connection with the murder of thirty-five year old widow Julia Mitchell gave himself up this afternoon, as the police net was closing in on his hiding-place. He is currently helping the police with their enquiries, and no charges have yet been made."

Film of Thorpe Wood came up, with policemen searching.

"A large section of the search party returned to normal duty this morning, but police did continue to search for what was described as vital evidence. However, this search was called off at lunchtime. A police presence is being maintained in the area to prevent any possible evidence being tampered with.

"Inspector David Lloyd spoke to Mel Brown this afternoon."

Inspector Lloyd mouthed silently at the camera for some moments. The film jerked and came to a standstill, and the newscaster appeared, unaware that he was on camera.

He looked up, under his eyebrows, quickly, then down again. Then, with studied confidence, he lifted his head again.

"I'm sorry, we seem to have some trouble with the sound on that film. We'll come back to it if we can. The police say that they are still anxious to hear from anyone who was in the Thorpe Wood area of Stansfield on Saturday night, and they would like to hear from the driver of a dark, open sports car which was seen at about nine o'clock on the night of the murder."

A blown-up fuzzy photograph of Julia smiled out at Helen from the screen.

"Police have issued this photograph of the murdered

woman, which they say was taken some time ago. Mrs.
Mitchell was wearing a denim skirt and jacket . . ."

Helen switched off the television. They weren't convinced it was Chris, then. They couldn't be, or they wouldn't be going to all this trouble.

But they didn't seem to be looking for anyone else.

"Ah yes, Inspector. You wanted to know a bit more about the time of death, I believe?" The pathologist's polite Glasgow voice sounded slightly condescending, but pleasant enough.

Lloyd, taking a breather from questioning, had decided to check the details more thoroughly, since Wade's insistence that she was alive when he left was fairly convincing.

"That's right," he said. "Is there likely to be any leeway?" Lloyd had reserved a corner of the blotter for notes on the conversation.

"No, I'm afraid not. I've given you what I consider to be the minimum and maximum. Thought you'd got him, didn't you?"

"Well, we're questioning someone. He's quite ready to admit that he left her after nine o'clock, but he insists that she was in robust health." Lloyd paused. "Is it possible for someone to have killed her after nine o'clock?"

"She was dead by nine o'clock, Inspector. Well dead, if you ask me."

Lloyd looked across at Judy, listening on the extension. "It's just that I don't want some clever dick turning up at the trial and throwing in a reasonable doubt." There was no question of that; Wade couldn't prove where he was after nine o'clock either, but it sounded better than admitting that you believed your suspect for no good reason.

"There isn't one, in my opinion. And I think you'd be hard pressed to find anyone to disagree."

"But pathologists have been known to disagree about time of death," Lloyd said. "I don't want that to happen, if possible."

"Oh, of course they have. It isn't an exact science—far

from it. You have to piece together what happened from what you know, what you can deduce—and what you can guess.'' He warmed to his task. ''As you no doubt know, you arrive at the time of death using several factors. Body temperature is the most reliable—rigor is the least.''

''And in this case?''

''In this case we had the added advantage of knowing when she last ate. But all these things are variables. Body temperatures for instance. A dead body loses heat, obviously, but in this case it would gain heat after death. Asphyxiation sends the body temperature up, and then it starts to fall. And there was quite an extreme drop in the outside temperature during that night—plus the fact that it was raining very heavily.'' He coughed, a deep, bronchial, smoker's cough. ''But you'll know all about that,'' he said. ''From other cases.''

''Some of it,'' Lloyd said guardedly. ''But it is the first murder-case I've taken charge of where there was any doubt at all. Both the others have pleaded guilty to manslaughter, thank God.''

Girvan laughed. ''Well,'' he said, through the hacking cough that the laugh had produced, ''as long as I'm not teaching my grandmother to suck eggs.'' He finished coughing, and continued. ''We know certain things. When she last ate, when she was last seen alive—that sort of thing. The stomach is a good guide—but its emptying process can be affected by a number of things, too.''

Lloyd was beginning to wish he'd never asked. ''I'm not over-keen on stomachs,'' he said, with a little laugh.

''Don't worry. All I mean is that if we just took that as a guide, it could give us too early a time of death. But the emotions experienced by the deceased come into the reckoning then. Fear slows the whole process down. So, you allow more time from when she ate.''

Lloyd could hear him flicking over pages.

''I believe she'd been having an argument with someone— if she was angry, that would speed the process up—but I think it's fairly safe to assume that there would be a considerable element of fear, from the circumstances.''

"Wouldn't there always be? If someone has been murdered?"

"Yes. I imagine there would. Once they know what's happening. No, I mean over a period of time."

"She was seen at about half past eight," Lloyd said. "We're told she looked scared then—I have to admit we were a bit dubious about that."

"Ah," Girvan said. "That seems quite likely from what we know. And taking everything into consideration, she had been dead for over ten and under twelve hours, which brings you to the times I gave you."

"But are you saying that it couldn't have happened at five past nine?"

"She was dead by nine o'clock, Inspector—and that's stretching it as far as I can. I'd be happier with 8:45 myself, but I allowed a bit more. But not after nine—definitely not."

He was rather more prepared to commit himself than most, which was something, Lloyd thought.

"Thank you for your time," he said. "I just wanted to be sure it couldn't have been later."

"No. Even if you assume that she was angry, which is the only question mark, that would make it earlier rather than later." He coughed again, and Lloyd could feel his own chest tightening.

"If your man was with her from—what was it?" He took the opportunity to cough while he obviously flicked the pages back again. "Half past eight until nine? Then he killed her, Inspector—or he was there when someone else did."

Lloyd replaced the receiver, and stood up. "I'll have another go," he said to Judy, and walked back down the corridor. He had meant to ask if she'd seen the news, but he might see her later. He pushed open the door of the interview room. "Tell me again," he said, removing his jacket, and hanging it over the back of the seat. "From when you went into the café."

Christopher James Wade sat at the table, his NHS crutch leaning against it, his plastered foot sticking out uncomfortably, telling the same story every time.

"I went in with her and shone the torch round. A table had been knocked over, I said how did that happen, she said she knocked it over in the dark." It was said in a sing-song, here-we-go-again fashion. Lloyd was seized with a fortunately controlled desire to kick his bad foot.

"Keep going—I'll stop you when I want more detail."

Wade glared at him. "I picked it up. I started looking for her pen, and she said it was all right, she hadn't really left her pen there at all." He fiddled with the signet ring that he wore on his little finger. "I said why were we there, and she said because she didn't want to go back to the Mitchells. I said why, and she said she'd rather be with me."

Lloyd, tired of the view of the town centre closing down for the night, walked slowly across to Wade. "And what did you think of that?" he asked wearily.

"I didn't know what to think."

"Well, then—" Lloyd sat down. "What did you say?"

"I said she hadn't given me that impression earlier." Wade tried to arrange his long legs more comfortably. "And she said that it wasn't a compliment—just that I was the lesser of two evils. I asked her what she meant, and she started going on about Helen. It ended up with a slanging match, and I left."

For a long time, Lloyd didn't speak, but Wade could play at that game too. "O.K.," he said, running a hand over his face. "I'm going to have something to eat. And I'll tell the canteen to rustle something up for you to eat. And we are both going to eat whatever it is we get, and then I'll come back, and you can tell me it all again."

"I am *not* going through all that again!" Wade shouted. "I've told you twice—that's it. I don't have to speak to you!"

"No, you don't. I told you that, remember? You don't have to say anything, but anything you do say will be written down and may be given in evidence. You say you don't want a solicitor—fine. But you are not telling me the truth, so if you do say anything when I come back it won't just be the same again. You'll be telling me the truth this time."

"I am telling you the truth!"

"Then why were you hiding out in a workmen's hut running with damp, used by all the animals in Christendom, making yourself ill? Why? Because you'd had a difference of opinion with someone?"

"Because you were after me for killing her!" Wade hid his face. "Because I was drunk, and I couldn't be sure."

"Sure of what?"

"If I'd—I was drunk! I just ran, that's all."

"From what, Mr. Wade?" Lloyd leant forward. "How did you know there was anything to run from?"

"I—" Wade looked bewildered. "The radio—they said . . ."

"We were at your garage and your house by half past six in the morning, It wasn't on the radio until much later."

Wade, tight-lipped, just shook his head.

"I went to see her in-laws," Lloyd continued conversationally. "Shortly after she was found. When I arrived, there were three mugs on the coffee table." He smiled friendlily at Wade. "It was odd, that—struck me at the time. She—Helen Mitchell—said that they were the previous night's. Now me, I'd leave last night's washing up—but her? I couldn't see it myself. But then it got curiouser and curiouser. See—she had this friend staying with her. No—I tell a lie—she was visiting, just for the day. But Julia Mitchell was there too. That made four of them. Then her husband and Julia go off—that just leaves two. Then she takes her friend to the station, and she's in on her own. Then her husband comes back—and that makes two again."

Wade wasn't dreadfully impressed.

"You see? There was no time when there were only three people in the house."

"There's no law against not having coffee," Wade said.

"None. Except that we know Julia did—I won't go into that, it's a bit upsetting—and I know her friend did, because I got the local police to ask, despite their thinking I was a bit tapped. And she said 'I had a visitor' to explain them—why there were three, and not just two. So that suggested herself, her husband and—you?"

Wade just sat there.

"That's how you knew, isn't it? Because I was at the door, telling them she was dead and that I was looking for you. Isn't it?"

"No."

"Then the only other explanation is that you knew she was dead because you killed her. Which do you prefer?"

With that, Lloyd went off in search of food, and found Judy in the canteen, in solitary splendour.

"Are you still here?" he asked, joining her.

"No, I went home half an hour ago. I've had Donald Mitchell touting for business, and three people who were nowhere near the area at the time, and—" she broke off. "You didn't catch the 5:45 news?"

"No. I was with Wade—how did it go?"

She caught her lip. "I don't know how to tell you this, really."

She looked suspiciously as though she were going to laugh. Lloyd narrowed his eyes. "What?"

"Well—"

He tried not to look too disappointed when she told him. He'd never hear the end of it if he did. It was difficult to know how to look. Laughing it off as though he was on television every night would produce much the same result.

"Not a word?"

She shook her head. "They didn't fit you in later, I'm afraid." And with that, the self-control snapped, and she began to laugh. "I'm sorry," she said, with difficulty. "I really am—it was just—of all the things to—"

And her laughter began to make him laugh, until the two of them were giggling like school-girls. It was brought to a sudden and not entirely successful halt by the appearance of more customers, when they tried to behave like dignified officers of the law.

"Do you want to sit in on the rest of this interview?" he asked, when order was restored. "Someone else there—a different approach. Just ask any questions that occur to you."

"Yes, I would like to—just kick me if you want me to shut up."

"I'll remember that," Lloyd promised.

"Why won't he have a solicitor?" Donald demanded.

Helen carried on laying the table in what seemed to Donald to be a particularly annoying fashion. "Because he didn't do it," she said calmly.

"All right! He didn't do it—that's no reason to refuse a solicitor. Solicitors aren't just for defending the guilty, you know! Why in God's name wouldn't he just ask for one?"

"Why are you behaving as though it was my fault?" Helen asked, reasonably enough.

Donald picked up the paper. "It's so stupid," he said. "Of all the people in the world—no one needs a solicitor like Chris Wade does now."

"Why?" Helen put down the place mats. "If he's done nothing wrong?"

"For Christ's sake, Helen—you know what he's like. He's never had to stand on his own two feet in his life. First it was his big sister, then it was Carrie, then it was me—" He folded the paper firmly. "Then it was you—let's not beat about the bush. He's always needed someone to lean on—and now, now of all times, he's got to play the hero."

"If he's got nothing to hide—"

Donald closed his eyes. Heaven only knew what he was telling them. "He has got something to hide," he said. "He was here—and we lied to the police. You know him as well as I do." He smiled. "You know him rather better than I do," he amended. "He'll be telling all sorts of stories to cover up for us. And he'll be making matters worse every time he opens his mouth."

Helen sat down opposite him. "So it isn't concern for Chris that's got you all hot and bothered?"

"No it isn't. I'm a solicitor! I can't get mixed up in this sort of thing. If he'd just asked for me—anyone—it wouldn't be so bad."

"But if he didn't do it."

Donald despaired of her. She really thought that if you didn't do it, there was nothing to worry about.

"Look—he was in there with her. We know that, because he told us. The police know it. He practically forced her to take a lift with him—and then he ran away, and she was found strangled. If he didn't do it, it hardly matters. The police have evidence that says he did. And he needs a solicitor to produce evidence that says he didn't."

"You could try again."

"And get touting for business added to my list of offences? No thanks. I went as a friend, to see if I could help, and I was told I couldn't. So that's that."

He tried reading the paper, but that hardly took his mind off it, since that was the lead story.

Judy looked at the tired, dispirited figure sitting at the table, the remains of his meal pushed away from him.

"The tea's good," she said. "Don't let it get cold."

Wade looked at her, his eyes dull. "Is this where you're nice to me and he's not?" he asked, nodding in Lloyd's direction. "I've seen that on the telly."

"No," Judy replied. "Nothing like that. It's where I explain to you that if you didn't kill Mrs. Mitchell, then you'd better start telling us the truth, so that we can work out what did happen. If you did kill her, then you'd better explain the circumstances, so that you've got some sort of defence."

"And you care, do you? Whether I've got a defence?"

"No. But you should—if not for your own sake, then for your friends'—like Helen Mitchell, for instance."

"What about her?" Wade drank some of his tea. "You're right," he said. "It is good."

"Hot and strong," Lloyd said. "Like love."

"Speaking about love," Judy said, as she felt she was being prompted to, "Mrs. Mitchell's very fond of you, isn't she?"

"Is she?" was the only response.

"Fond enough to tell lies for you." Judy drank some of her own tea. "She had to tell the truth in the end, though—

but she did try." She glanced at Lloyd, who had got up and was standing by the window. Wade saw the glance.

"You're the one that's telling lies," he said.

"No, not me," Judy said. "She has admitted that she saw you."

They weren't getting anywhere like this. "What was your row with Julia about?"

"Helen."

"She seems to have been in a particularly argumentative mood. Having rows with everyone—did she say what her row with Donald was about?"

"No." Wade looked surprised, as though it was the first time he'd thought about it. "No, she didn't."

"Why did you go to your garage when you left? Why didn't you go home, or back to your sister's?"

Lloyd had wandered back to the table, and was standing behind Wade, who had twisted round in an effort to see him. "I was in a bit of a state," he said.

"Why?" Lloyd asked. "Because you'd had a row with Julia?"

"Yes."

"A total stranger? Why should having a row with her bother you?"

Wade turned back to Judy. "It wasn't the row—not really. It was the accident."

Lloyd walked slowly round to face him. "What accident?"

"Oh—it wasn't really an accident—but it reminded me of the accident. That's what made me get drunk."

"Reminded you?" Lloyd said. "Of what—your wife's accident?"

He nodded briefly.

"What happened to remind you?" Judy asked, as Lloyd took up his post by the window again.

"Something ran in front of the car as I was going up to the café. I braked, and she fell forward—she didn't hurt herself, but she could have—I swore I'd never do that again."

"And that upset you?"

116

"Of course! It was just the same—she could have been hurt. I thought I'd never do that again, and I did. I did exactly the same thing!" He turned his head away.

Lloyd crossed behind him, and went out of the room.

"Your wife died and she didn't—was that what it was?" Judy said carefully. "You felt angry before you ever went into the café with her?"

"No!"

"But she didn't want you to wait for her—why did you insist on going in with her?"

"I wanted to take her to Helen's—I told you!" He made to jump up, and the constable whose name Judy could never remember leapt to his feet. But Wade winced and sat down again, reaching for his crutch.

"Why? She was a grown woman—she didn't want you."

Wade shook his head quickly. "You make it sound as though I forced her—it wasn't like that. She said not to wait for her, and I said of course I would—that was all." He stood up, this time with the aid of the crutch. "Do you mind?" he asked. "I'll get cramp if I have to sit there."

"Not at all."

He took a deep breath. "All right—I wanted to see Helen. Donald was out of the way, and taking her back was a good excuse. If I left her there I didn't have any reason to go to the Mitchells' house. But when I got in there, she said she didn't want to go back. At first she said it was because she'd had a row with Donald and she didn't want to see anyone until she'd calmed down. So I picked up the table and said we should sit down for a moment."

Lloyd came back in, with more tea. "Thought we could do with some more," he said cheerily. "It looks as though it's going to be a long night."

"At first?" Judy repeated. "What did she say after that?"

"Nothing much. She sat down, but she—she looked *scared*. Or cold. But it was so hot, I didn't think she could be cold. Then I thought she might not be feeling well—''flu, or something. I took off my jacket, and said if she was cold she should put it on."

117

Judy wrote SCARED on her ever-present notebook, and leafed back through the pages to Diane's evidence. *She looked a bit scared,* it read.

"Scared of you?" she asked.

Wade sat down again, easing himself on to the chair, almost falling, as his crutch crashed down to the floor. "I didn't think so," he said. "She had no reason to be." He retrieved the crutch.

"Scared or cold," Lloyd said. "That's what you said, isn't it?"

"Yes." Wade looked at him sullenly. "It could have been either."

"What was she doing that made you think that?"

"She kept her arms folded," Wade said.

"Her arms folded?" Judy repeated.

"Yes," Wade said. "She was standing there with her arms folded. Even when she sat down, she kept them folded."

"Folded how?" Lloyd sat down beside Judy. "Show me."

Wade obliged, folding his arms as they had all been told to at school. "You know," he said.

"And she did make you angry?"

"Yes. We sat there for a few moments—then I offered her my jacket, but she didn't want it. I tried to talk to her—just small talk, but she didn't want to know. So I asked if she was feeling all right."

"And?"

"She said she'd feel better if I would just go. And I said if she didn't feel well, she should let me take her back to Helen's."

"How long do you think you'd been in there at this point?" Judy asked.

"About ten minutes or so. And she said I should go if that's what I wanted. To Helen's, I mean. She said she knew about us. She said Donald knew."

Lloyd sat back, tipping the chair dangerously on its back legs, and Judy braced herself for the crash that fortunately didn't come.

"Knew what?" Lloyd asked.

118

"There's nothing to know," Wade said. "That's just it. Helen isn't like her—she doesn't—" he broke off.

Neither Judy nor Lloyd spoke. Wade had at last given up his attempt to say nothing, and they could just sit back and let him go.

"She started going on about her. I said she wouldn't understand about someone like Helen. They'd told me about her—Helen had, and Donald. No wonder someone killed her. She said I only wanted to run her back so that I could—" he stopped, his eyes perplexed. "She was very crude," he said to Judy. "I don't want to repeat what she said."

"All right," she said, amiably.

"I told her that it wasn't like that. It's not!" he said, looking from one to the other. Helen believes in marriage vows—she won't break them!"

Judy cast a sidelong glance at Lloyd.

"So that just made her worse. She started laughing at me, and telling me to get out and get on with it. She said Helen would be grateful—and in the end she was nearly hysterical—just telling me to get out, so I did."

Lloyd was drinking his tea unconcernedly when Wade finished his story. He set down the mug, and looked at him. "That was when you killed her, was it?" he asked quietly.

"I didn't—she was perfectly all right when I left. She was all right—she said she was!"

Judy looked up sharply from her notebook. "Said she was?"

Wade had gone pale. "I mean—she was all right."

"Why did she say she was?"

"I didn't mean that—I meant—" He closed his eyes.

"When did she hit her head on the table?" Lloyd asked.

He opened his eyes again, and frowned. "She didn't," he said.

"Well, there was a cut on her face. Her blood was on the table. Varnish from the table was in the cut. What conclusion would you come to?"

"But she didn't hurt herself—she wasn't bleeding."

Lloyd stood up. "No, not much. That's because she was dead, Mr. Wade. But you seem not to have noticed that."

"She wasn't! She wasn't dead!"

"Why was she naked?" Judy asked suddenly.

Wade looked slowly from Lloyd to her. "Naked?" he said. "She wasn't. She wasn't naked, and she wasn't dead."

"She was mad at Donald Mitchell with whom she'd been having an affair," Lloyd said. "You gave her a lift, and she saw her chance to get her own back on Donald. She took you up there, led you on a bit—why was she naked? I had a theory—you remember?" He turned to Judy, who wasn't sure what her reaction should be. "I didn't go into it at the time, but it could be right. It was hot—very hot. Right?" he asked Wade.

Wade, bewildered, agreed.

"And there was the boating lake—what was it? Let's have a swim? And you chickened out? Or did you both strip off, and then things developed, and you couldn't cope? You decided to call it a day—and she laughed at you? Was that when she made you angry? Was that when you killed her?"

Wade sat with his head in his hands, saying nothing. When he sat up, it was with a new kind of assurance.

"She was fully clothed, and alive, when I left. She did say she was all right. The reason she said that was that I had *asked* her if she was."

"In the middle of a row?"

"No. The row ended when I pushed her."

"Don't tell me we're getting to the truth at last," Lloyd said. "You pushed her. When?"

"When she had gone too far. I pushed her away, then I apologised, and asked if she was all right. She shouted yes, and ran into the boatshed. I followed her in there, and I said I was sorry, because I could see I'd frightened her, and I didn't mean to. But she was nearly hysterical. She had the phone in her hand, and she said she would call the police if I didn't leave. So I left."

"How hard did you hit her?"

120

"I *didn't* hit her. I pushed her, that's all, and she stumbled and ran away."

"Was her face cut?" Judy asked.

Wade didn't know. "It could have been—you could hardly see in there. We only had the torch. I don't think it was."

"It was," Lloyd assured him. "Did she fall against the table? Was that when it got knocked over?"

"No. I've told you about the table."

Judy decided it was her turn to stretch her legs, and took a slow turn round the room as she formulated her next question. "You left her there," she said. "Alive?"

There was a small exasperated noise from Wade.

"Holding the phone, you said." Judy looked out through the rain-flecked window to the town and its closed shops. The lit windows of Stansfield's only hotel made her wish she was in there, sipping gin and tonic, relaxing. "Without leaving her fingerprints?"

Lloyd took over. "And then you went where?"

"To the garage," Wade said wearily. "And I got drunk." His shoulders sagged. "That's what I do best," he muttered.

"And then you went to Helen Mitchell's like you'd wanted to all along?" Judy said.

"Yes."

"Did you tell her what had happened?"

"I don't know. I don't remember much about it."

Lloyd stood up, scraping the chair back on the floor. "I think we should all sleep on it," he said, and the constable stood up.

Judy watched as Chris limped away, supported by the constable on one side, and his crutch on the other.

"What do you think?" she asked.

Lloyd stretched. "I think we should go home." He smiled. "I didn't have time to collect the car—what with the interview, and this—" he lifted his hands helplessly.

They were both too pre-occupied to chat as they collected their things from the office, and drove home in near silence. Judy tried to cast Wade in the role of murderer, and couldn't. He didn't seem to know how she'd died, or he was very good

121

at keeping his wits about him. She signalled, ready to pull into the garage area behind the flats.

"You don't have to," Lloyd said, as the car's lights swept over the garage doors. "I could have—"

"—nipped through the alley," Judy finished the sentence with him. "I know." She switched off the engine, and they were plunged in darkness as she flicked the light switch. "It might not solve anything," she said, kissing him lightly on the lips. "But it would cheer me up no end."

Lloyd laughed. "The Superintendent won't like it," he said, feeding her the line.

"The Superintendent," Judy said obediently, "isn't getting it."

The rabbit saw the headlights, and stopped dead, staring at them. The car drew slowly to a halt, then moved right. The rabbit moved to his left, and the car stopped again.

The rabbit wasn't going to run. He had tried that the other night, and he'd nearly got run over. He was just going to sit there until the car went away.

The car moved back to its left. The rabbit moved to his right, and the car stopped again.

Then the lights weren't there, so the car must have gone. The rabbit raced to the other side of the road, on to the safe grass, away from the cars.

The young policeman put his lights on again, and moved off down the road, where the "police presence" was being maintained. He didn't know why they were making all this fuss. They'd got him.

He was caught, like the rabbit in the headlights.

CHAPTER NINE

COULD HE HAVE KILLED HER? CHRIS TOSSED around on the bunk, wishing he could sleep and forget the whole thing for a few hours. The more he tried to tell them his story, the more likely it seemed that he *had* killed her. Could there have been any time he didn't remember? He went through everything again in his head. Driving her home, taking her up there, going in with her, picking up the table, sitting down, talking to her, arguing with her, losing his temper, pushing her, *pushing* her, not hitting her. Could she have hurt herself then? Was it possible for someone to run away, pick up a phone, speak—no, of course it wasn't. But if she did hit her head—but he could swear she didn't hurt herself at all. He left her standing there, holding the phone. He went back to the garage, got drunk—he even had hazy memories of talking to the milk-lady. Staggering off to Helen, and then—then, there was a memory gap. He didn't know how long he was at the garage, how long he was with Helen— he didn't know if he'd gone straight to Helen's.

They said Donald had been having an affair with Julia. Since when? Donald couldn't stand the sight of her as far as Chris knew, and anyway, he boasted about his women. Surely it was whats-her-name—Julia's lady-in-waiting—that he was having the affair with. It had been going on a long time. Helen thought it was Julia—she told him that night, under the impression that Donald's behaviour was news to him. He hadn't corrected her—how could he? Oh, but she wouldn't *kill* Julia, would she? Even if she thought . . . would she?

Judy had thought she might feel guilty, but she didn't. Perhaps that came tomorrow—perhaps it didn't come at all. She felt warm and happy, and glad she'd made her mind up. Lloyd had opened a decadent bottle of wine, and it was just beginning to go to her head as they sat up in bed to finish it off.

"Thank you for having me," she whispered, then giggled at her own wit.

"I was wrong," he said, reaching over her for her glass. "The Superintendent would like it."

She laughed. "You forgot to talk like Richard Burton," she said. "Did you know? Or is the boy from the valleys just another character part?"

"I don't know." He poured more wine into her half-full glass. "It must be—I'm not from the valleys."

"Oh," she said sympathetically. "Do you mean you can't go on about pit disasters and washing your father's back in the bath in front of the kitchen fire?"

He grinned. "I can go on about anything. It's not very often true."

"Where are you from?"

"Somewhere even I can't pronounce." He drank his wine down like water. "Fishing village—I'd have been a fisherman if we'd stayed."

"What age were you when you moved to Stansfield?"

"Fourteen." He sighed. "Thirty years ago this week, near as makes no difference."

"What's your first name?"

"Ah, no—you don't get me like that. You'll have to get me drunk—and this stuff won't do it."

"You told the television people it was David. It's not David. Why would you mind people knowing that?"

She sipped her wine, since it was having rather more effect on her than it was on Lloyd. "Would you have liked being a fisherman?"

"Not me. I'm too fond of my creature comforts." His lips touched her hair. "I'll stick to being a fisher of men."

"My God, I'll bet that is how you see yourself, isn't it?" Judy shook her head. "St. Peter—that's your name, is it?"

"Different line, different bait—different catch."

She groaned, and drained her wine glass though she hadn't really meant to.

"Have some more," he said, the bottle poised over her glass.

She covered it with her hand. "No thank you—I've got to sober up enough to drive home."

"You don't have to drive home!" But he put the bottle down, and lay back. "You want me to throw Wade back, don't you?"

"Hark who never discusses business when he's finished work!" She thought for a moment. "Is this a private metaphor, or can anyone join?"

"Feel free." He put his arm round her and pulled her closer. "Let's have your angle."

She dug him in the ribs. "All right. We've got more than one fish in the net. We've only got Helen Mitchell's word for it that she hung about at the station. She could have left sharp, and been at the boating lake before nine o'clock."

Lloyd shifted round the better to look quizzically at her. "So what?"

"She could have seen Wade's car go up there. She could have seen it from the house, or on her way to the station. She could have got her friend on to the train and got back there. Gone up to see what was going on—and found that Julia had got her hooks into Chris as well as her husband. She wouldn't be too happy, would she?"

Lloyd made a disbelieving noise, and she sat up, twisting out of his arms. "Why not?"

"For one thing she was strangled. That takes strength."

"Helen Mitchell's no weakling—and Julia wasn't what you'd call robust, was she?"

Lloyd frowned. "But then what? Undressed her?"

"To make it look like a man had done it. Or maybe she

125

didn't have to—maybe she interrupted them at just the wrong moment. Wade runs off—leaving his jacket—and Helen finishes Julia's game for her.''

"But how did she manage all that without leaving one shred of evidence? And why hide her clothes?''

Judy didn't have an answer for that. But it fitted. Wade's shirt was unbuttoned when the milkwoman saw him, which could have meant he'd had to dress hurriedly. His reluctance to bring Helen into it all—the pathologist's suggestion that he could have seen the murder. She lay back down again.

"Any more theories?'' Lloyd asked.

"Mitchell—he came into a lot of money.''

"Mitchell was with Wade's own sister, who would swear black was white if it got her brother off.'' He leant over. "And before you start talking about hit-men and the like, think about it.''

Judy pushed him away. "I had no intention of talking about hit-men.''

He looked suitably abashed. "I thought about it. But since only Julia knew she was going up there, she'd have had to co-operate. That seems unlikely. Unless the said hit-man was Wade, of course, in which case he could have forced her up there.''

"And hypnotised her into leaving the Shorts' house early,'' Judy said matter-of-factly. "That's the answer, of course. How clever of you.''

"That's what I meant. Even I entertained the idea until I realised it was nonsense.''

"Even you! Well, that's all right, then. I'm not such a silly little girl after all.'' She helped herself to the rest of the wine. What in the world was she doing? Had she really wished this on herself? "I must be mad,'' she said. "Even talking to you.''

"I didn't mean it like that—I—oh, to hell. I'm going to get a proper drink!'' He put on a dressing-gown that she would have remarked on, if she had been speaking to him.

He was gone a long time; long enough for her to have finished the wine, read an article in Punch, and missed him.

He reappeared, carrying a tray with two steaming mugs. "Coffee," he said. "Black and strong, so that you can sober up as requested." He handed her a mug, and got into bed.

"Thank you," she said automatically, absently. She blew at the steam, and tested it carefully. "It's too hot," she said, and watched with horror as he took a deep drink. "Your mouth must be asbestos," she said, putting her mug down to cool.

His mouth, still hot from the coffee, was on hers. "You taste nice," she said. "Like Gaelic coffee." She pulled away. "You haven't put whisky in mine, have you?"

"No." He held up three fingers. "Scout's Honour."

She tested it all the same, but it seemed to be innocent of alcohol.

"It could have been two people," Lloyd said reflectively. "The underwear puzzles me. Why would you roll up her clothes and stash them in one place, and bundle up her underwear and hide it yards away in the opposite direction?"

"But even if it was two people—I mean, let's say it was Helen, and Wade saw her and helped her cover it up—why would one person take her outer clothing and the other her under-clothing? If they were going to strip her, wouldn't one person do it, and hide it?" Judy picked up her coffee again. "Why take her clothes off at all?"

"Why do people take their clothes off?" Lloyd asked.

"To have a bath," Judy said.

"To swim?" Lloyd laughed. "I think that's a non-starter, really. No one in their right mind would swim in that boating lake."

"To discuss murder-cases," Judy suggested with a grin.

They put down the coffee mugs and lay back. Judy pulled pensively at the hairs on his chest until he yelped. "Sorry," she said, smoothing them down again. "Lloyd?"

"Present."

"Were you ever unfaithful to Barbara?" she asked, not sure of what reaction the question would get.

"Yes," he said promptly. "Once. Brief and inglorious."

He laughed. "She was a rank and file violinist with the BBC Symphony Orchestra."

"Are you making that up?"

"No. That's what she was—I always imagine them being drilled. 'Shoulder violins! Play, two three four.' "

Judy sat up, leaning on her elbow, looking down at him. "Did you feel guilty?" she demanded.

"A bit. Yes, I did. I think that's why it didn't last very long." He touched her cheek. "Why? Do you?"

Judy shook her head, and her hand went to his. "I should," she said, smiling suddenly. "So let's try again and see if it makes me feel guilty this time."

The gales of the night before dominated News at Ten, and Chris was relegated to a mention in the closing stages, before the sport. Donald watched it all without seeing a thing. Another hour passed before he decided not to wait for Helen, who had obviously decided that she was no longer under any obligation to keep him posted about her movements, and had got up and gone out after dinner without a word. She'd be at Elaine's, of course. He knew that without checking up. They could both sit and worry about Chris, as though that did any good. A trouble shared was a trouble exacerbated, in Donald's book.

He switched off the television, and went to bed. Busy day tomorrow—he'd have to start making arrangements to leave. They'd want as much notice as possible, to give them time to find a replacement. And he wanted to start looking through the properties currently on Mitchell Development's books. He was in the market for good premises in a reasonably fashionable area.

"I can't stay," Judy said, pulling on her tights. "My car's outside—people have very suspicious minds you know. They might think we were sleeping together."

Lloyd laughed. "Who's going to see it?" He sat up and tried to catch her arm, but she pulled it away.

"WPC Alexander, for one," she said. "She lives in the

flats behind this block." She zipped up her skirt. "Where are my shoes?" She looked round the room, and under the bed, and then went out into the living room.

Lloyd put on his dressing-gown, and followed her, shivering slightly as his bare feet hit the tiles in the hallway.

"Mary?" he said. "She wouldn't say a word. Anyway—you could have been spending the night with her."

She found her shoes. "These days that would cause even more talk," she said, laughing. "Got them." She held them up, and saw his dressing-gown.

"You look stunning, my dear," she said, holding on to him as she put her shoes on. "Are you wearing that for a bet?"

Lloyd rather liked it, with its gold dragons on a maroon background. "It was a present," he lied, because he had bought it himself the year they went to Tenerife.

"Was it? Don't expect one like that from me, will you?"

"I don't expect a thing," he said, putting his arms 'round her.

She kissed him, her tongue gently seeking his. "I've got to go," she whispered.

"Some more coffee," he said. "Make sure you're sober. Maybe you're not—you don't want to be caught drunk in charge, do you?"

He could feel her giving in. "All right. One cup of coffee." She took out her cigarettes.

"Oh good," Lloyd said. "I was afraid that this wasn't an occasion."

He made the coffee, humming to himself. She might stay, if he pointed out to her that it was almost midnight and WPC Alexander would have already suspected that she hadn't come for a shilling for the meter. He found some biscuits that he didn't know he had, and piled them on to a plate.

"Coffee and biscuits," he announced, setting the tray down on the coffee table. "The biscuits are of a certain age—I don't really advise them."

"I'm hungry," she said, biting into one. "They're all right. A bit soft."

129

Lloyd sat beside her on the sofa. "You know how I never discuss work at home?" he said.

She smiled. "Go on—you're going to give me my timetable for tomorrow, aren't you?"

"You started it!"

"I did not," she said. "You mentioned Wade—I was talking about your childhood."

"So you were." He bit into a biscuit, but he couldn't agree with her as to their all rightness. He screwed up his face. "Don't eat these—I'll make you a sandwich if you're hungry."

"They're fine. But since you've brought the subject up again—what are you going to do about Helen Mitchell?"

"Randall says I should use my discretion," he said. "Assuming Wade's telling the truth, that is. She didn't know he would suddenly disappear as soon as she left him. And then she found herself in a difficult position." He shook his head. "One law for the rich."

"Oh, come on—that's fair enough. It's not as though she knew where he was."

"Do you think Superintendent Don't-You-Know-Who-I-Am Randall would have been as sweetly reasonable if it had been some little scrubber and her boyfriend?"

Maybe he would, Judy thought. She had a higher opinion of Randall than Lloyd did, but she didn't say so. "I think we should talk to her, all the same," she said. "About withholding information."

"And about nipping up and doing in her sister-in-law?" Lloyd asked.

"I could touch on that."

"We could: I want to see her too. After all, when you think about it, she wasn't so much losing a sister-in-law as gaining access to what Mitchell described as 'a considerable estate.' "

Judy solemnly finished her revolting biscuit, and washed it down. "I think he's telling the truth," she said.

Lloyd raised his eyebrows. "The whole truth?" he asked.

"If he isn't, he's very good. And the bit about the near miss is probably true—Diane heard his brakes squealing."

Lloyd knew what she meant, but there was no point in flying in the face of evidence. "We'll see what we can get from Mrs. Mitchell," he said. "Are we missing something? Is it wheelbarrows, do you think?"

"Wheelbarrows?"

"Man wheeling a wheelbarrow covered with a tarpaulin out of a building site. The foreman stops him, looks under the tarpaulin, but it's empty. So he has to let him go. The man does the same thing every day for six weeks, until the job's finished.

"On the last day, the foreman stops him, says he won't shop him, but will he please put him out of his misery, and tell him what he's been stealing, because he knows he's been stealing something. And the man says—"

"Wheelbarrows," Judy finished, smiling. "But what could we be missing?"

"Perhaps there's a glaringly obvious reason for taking her clothes off—with care, the report said. Her clothes were removed with care."

"With care." Judy thought for a moment. "So she didn't divest herself in a mad passion." She leant back, her head on his shoulder, and he smiled to himself.

"Love, oh love, oh careful love," he said. "And he didn't tear them off in a frenzy. Someone took them off *with care*, then someone rolled them up and hid them. Why?"

"To delay identification?" Judy suggested.

"It didn't work. Her bag was there, anyway—with letters and credit cards. Not to mention a reminder from her dentist in case we had to identify her by her teeth." He laughed. "As cunning ruses go, that one wasn't so good."

"Even if he was stupid enough to think that we'd fall for rape—he'd surely have just messed her clothes about? Torn them, that sort of thing?" Judy got herself more comfortable. "And if he was going to hide them, or set fire to them—why roll them all up together like that? Wouldn't you just pick them up?"

"I think they were thrown," Lloyd said. "From the car, as it left. They would land about there from the pathway. Then the shoes." His arm was beginning to go to sleep, and he shifted slightly. "But why stuff her underwear into the roots of a tree?"

"You didn't tell me that bit," she said, twisting round.

Lloyd exercised his arm to bring the circulation back. "Oh, sorry. Yes, stuffed into the roots of a tree." He rubbed his eyes. "And I thought we'd have all the answers once we spoke to Wade—if you ask me, he's as much in the dark as we are."

Judy grinned triumphantly. "Hah! You don't think he killed her."

"No, I don't. But Randall says we'll have to charge him tomorrow if we're no further forward, and for once I think he's right. We've got an eye-witness, fingerprints, the time—his own behaviour. We can't ignore all that."

"Then we'll just have to give Mrs. M. a fright," she said decidedly. "Let's talk to her on our own ground."

"Anything you say." He bent over to kiss her, but she slid deftly away from him.

"I'm going."

"What's the point? It's well after midnight—your reputation is in shreds, Mrs. Hill."

"I'm still going." She went to get her raincoat, and Lloyd found himself back in the café, trying to find the wheelbarrows. "He's lying about one thing," he said when she came back. "The phone—her fingerprints would have been on the phone, as you so rightly pointed out."

"Yes, I don't understand that. Why say it at all?"

"Well, we can see what sort of prints they did get from the phone," he said, following her to the door. "It's raining," he said.

"I'll survive." They kissed goodnight at the door, like teenagers, and he knew she didn't want to go any more than he wanted her to.

"Julia's prints are elusive," she whispered, stepping outside.

"The car door's stiff," he said. "The passenger can't do it unless they're used to it. I checked—it's true. And his prints bear him out."

"Everything," Judy said, kissing him again, "bears him out."

Lloyd watched her until she disappeared round the zig-zag of the pathway to the garages.

It was true. Everything did bear Wade's story out. The only conflicting evidence was the phone, which until now hadn't even come into the reckoning. Well, at least he could check that.

He heard Judy's car start up, and wished she had stayed.

Helen Mitchell was driving home late, too. She drove fast along Thorpe Wood Road, feeling better since her visit to Elaine. Insects danced in the lights, and died on her wind-screen as she drove, and she could see that the house was in darkness. She hadn't really meant to disappear all evening without telling Donald where she was going, but there was something about his attitude that she found hard to take.

All that seemed to be bothering him was that she had lied to the police, and that Chris might land them in it. Everything else—including Julia's death—he was quite happy to take in his stride. Everything else. And that irked her slightly, she told herself honestly. A little jealousy might have been in order. But he took that in his stride as well, because he'd been going to leave her anyway. As long as it didn't directly affect him, Donald didn't care what happened to anyone. She had tried to tell him about her interview with the sergeant, but he'd been too preoccupied to listen.

Still, Elaine seemed to think that the police weren't entirely hostile. She had even said that Sergeant Hill was nice, an adjective that had not leaped to Helen's mind when describing her. But it had made her feel better, and a little more as though she might come out of this business unscathed.

A cat, blacker than the night, streaked across the road as soon as the car had passed, skittering to a halt at the long grass, overdue for mowing. Above its yellowing fringe danced the daddy-long-legs, bathed in light from the road. The cat dabbed a curious paw at one or two, but she was after bigger game. She moved noiselessly through the grass, into the woods, stopping in the clearing where Paul and Diane had inexpertly consummated their union. She could have told them a thing or two about that, if they'd asked.

She stood motionless, then darted through the trees towards the building. She watched for a moment as the ducks swam away, but they weren't her prey. Into the trees again, and she was there. Invisible against the dark bark, she waited for the mice who would come to nibble the picnic leftovers.

She had to keep her strength up. She had kittens to feed. She washed unnecessarily, her sleek coat shining in the fitful moonlight, and settled down, her eyes closing now and again, but her ears prickled for the tiny sound of an unwitting mouse. She wouldn't miss a thing; she never did.

Oh yes. She could tell them a thing or two, if they asked.

CHAPTER TEN

JUDY WOKE BEFORE THE ALARM, AND LAY IN A DE-
licious state of semi-consciousness, sleepily aware that she
was happy. They had made each other laugh, she and Lloyd,
and the knowledge that they could just as easily make each
other cry made the laughter all the sweeter. She had laughed
at his need for words, but delighted in the sound of his voice,
by turns persuasive, funny, soothing, exciting. She had gone
home simply because he didn't want her to, and he had
laughed at her need for independence, but he hadn't tried too
hard to make her stay.

With deliberate perverseness they had steered the talk
round to work; the whispered doorstep conversation had been
about Wade, as though they were trying to assure one another
that it had all been just for fun. They needed the assurance,
because whatever way it had started out, and whatever way
it had ended, in between there had been an intensity of feeling that had caught them both unaware.

And she still didn't feel guilty. In fact, she thought drowsily, it was that which was making her happy, because she
had never felt like that before. She was glad she was on her
own, hugging her thoughts to herself with no temptation to
impart them to Lloyd.

The buzzer rudely invaded those private thoughts, and
dragged her reluctantly out into the day. The morning paper
screamed WOODLAND MURDER—MAN HELD at her.

135

Everyone did it—she did it. You heard that the police had someone helping them with their enquiries, and you thought "oh good, they've got him"—it was human nature, though not a particularly praiseworthy aspect of it. She ran her bath, reading the emotional, if not sensational words that accompanied the photograph of Superintendent Randall "leading the murder hunt." Murder Weapon Still Missing, read a smaller sub-heading. Woodland Hideout, read another. They knew nothing of Wade—nothing that they could print—and yet without a single libellous word, they managed to produce him to the public, gift-wrapped and guilty.

The morning routine began to take over; it was difficult to remain on a high philosophical plane with the smell of bacon and eggs teasing your nostrils. She ate rather more heartily than might be expected of someone entering a new phase of her life, and drove to work entirely restored to normality.

"Morning Sarge," Sandwell said as she walked in—an unusually colloquial greeting from him.

"Good morning, Bob—anything I should know about?"

"Forensic's report on the rest of Mrs. Mitchell's clothes," he said. "It's on Inspector Lloyd's desk, but he's not in yet."

"My God!" Judy said, startling him a little. Perhaps not entirely restored, she told herself. Freud would have been interested. "I think he might be expecting me to pick him up," she said. "Unless he's gone to fetch his car—I think it's ready now." She thought for a moment. "Why don't you give him a ring?" she said. "And I'll see if that report says anything interesting."

She left Sandwell to it, fighting the desire to laugh as she walked through the CID room with people in various stages of arriving, bidding them a cheerier good morning than they were used to.

Closing the office door behind her, she waited for the extension to ring, which it duly did.

"Did you do this on purpose?" Lloyd's voice demanded to know.

"No!" She laughed. "I swear I didn't—I'm sorry."

There was a small silence. "But that's *worse*," he said.

136

"No, it's not really. Do you want me to come and pick you up now?"

"No thank you," he said huffily. "Bob Sandwell's coming for me."

"I'm sorry," she said again, there being not a lot else to say. "I'll see you when you come in."

"Huh." And he hung up.

Judy replaced the receiver, and picked up the lab report on the underwear. Like the other clothes, it had merely been removed. Nothing to suggest whether it was before or after death, nothing to suggest forcible or violent removal. The tights had a small run, but that could have happened at any time. They were not the murder weapon.

Not the murder weapon. Everyone had assumed that they must have been, since they weren't found with her other clothes. She wondered if she should see Chief Inspector Royle about releasing men to continue the search, but decided against it. Lloyd might think otherwise, so for the moment she'd leave it. Whatever was used had probably been burned long ago, and it was unlikely to tell them much more than they already knew.

Lloyd came in a few minutes later, and agreed with her that there was little point in searching now, especially since the inch by inch search had yielded nothing.

There was an unspoken agreement that only work would be discussed during working hours. Lloyd stuck to this one, unlike the reverse agreement.

"I think we can take the barriers down," he said. "We're not going to learn any more there." He spoke to Randall, then arranged for the watch to be taken off the boating lake.

"What do you think?" he said. "Send a car and bring her in for questioning?"

"Yes," Judy said. "Let her get the wind up a bit."

Helen had just put away the breakfast dishes when the knock came to the door. Donald had left early to go to work, because he had missed a day. She had wondered a little about

137

that. She opened the door to an extremely tall, extremely young constable.

"Mrs. Helen Mitchell?"

"Yes," she said. "Can I help you?"

"It's in connection with your sister-in-law's death," he said, very formally. "Inspector Lloyd would like a word with you. At the police station," he added, slightly hesitantly, very politely.

"Now?"

"Yes, please, Mrs. Mitchell."

"I have already spoken to someone—a lady. A sergeant, I think." It was supposed to sound casual, unconcerned; it didn't.

"That would be Sergeant Hill," he said. "But Inspector Lloyd has a few more questions, if you wouldn't mind."

And if she did? Helen decided there was little to be gained from finding out, and got her handbag. She glanced up at the sky. She wouldn't need her coat. The sky, a bright jigsaw puzzle blue, held the promise of a warm, late summer day.

As she got into the car, she saw a neighbour's curtain twitch. What did they think of all this, all these polite people who had smiled good morning shyly since it had happened? What did they think of all the police cars, and the reporters still having to be repulsed? The ones she knew merely sympathised; the ones she didn't must wonder.

In no time, they were pulling into the station car-park, and she was being ushered up some steps into the building itself. She had never been inside a police station, a fact that only came home to her as she walked along the corridor. You would think that everyone would have been in one by the time they were fifty, she thought. But she couldn't remember ever having lost her bicycle, like the small boy at the desk. When her purse was stolen, she put it down to experience. That it had happened twice showed that she did not learn by her mistakes.

She followed the young man through a room with three empty desks, to an ante-room in which sat the sergeant who had so easily manipulated her, and Inspector Lloyd, only dimly remembered from the frantic moments of Sunday morning, a hundred years ago.

"Mrs. Mitchell. Do have a seat." It was the cool collected sergeant who spoke, extending her hand towards the empty chair in front of her desk. Helen glanced nervously at the inspector, but he was sorting papers, taking no apparent interest in her presence. She sat down, feeling like a child who has been sent for by the head.

"Thank you for coming in," the sergeant continued, as though she had had any choice in the matter. Though the constable hadn't said that she must come.

"Mrs. Mitchell, I got the impression from you that you want to help Mr. Wade in any way you can. Was I right?"

"He is a friend, as you pointed out," Helen said frostily.

"Quite. That's why it is important that you tell us the truth. I wonder if you are."

"I am not accustomed to having my word doubted," Helen said. It did annoy her, even if there was every reason to doubt it. "Do you object to my having a cigarette?"

"Not at all." The sergeant pushed the ashtray towards her with her pen.

Helen smoked nervously, still looking across at Lloyd now and again.

"You did leave one thing out when we spoke before," the sergeant said. "And I get the feeling that you have left rather more than that out."

Helen began to see what Donald meant. She had no idea what Chris had said to them—how much of the truth. She had no idea how much damage the truth would do, or if lying would just hammer the final nail in his coffin. She said nothing, and waiting for the next question.

"Where were you at five to nine on Saturday evening?" The question came, disconcertingly, from the inspector.

Helen twisted round. "I told Sergeant Hill," she said. "I was coming back from the station—I had to see someone to a train."

"Were you?" he said. "You see—you say you were. But you didn't get home until twenty-five to ten. It's—what? A five minute journey? Seven—eight at the very most. And it was a quiet night—well, it's a quiet road, isn't it? At night.''

"I've already explained—" Helen looked back at Sergeant Hill. "—the storm. I couldn't see where I was going." She tried to calm herself by drawing deeply on her cigarette.

"Yes," he said. "You parked in the lay-by."

"That's right."

"And did what, Mrs. Mitchell?" Sergeant Hill again.

"Nothing." She looked across at Lloyd. "Nothing," she said again, helplessly.

"You didn't go up to the café? Leave your car in the lay-by and go up to the café? Wasn't that where you saw Mr. Wade's car? Where you knew you would see it, because you'd seen him go in there on your way to the station?"

"No!" Helen had never imagined that this was why she had been brought here. "I told you where I saw his car."

"After some prompting," the sergeant said. "I think you saw his car at the boating lake—you went into the café to see what was going on, and you saw Wade kill your sister-in-law. I think you didn't get home until twenty-five to ten because you were helping him. Why did you hide her clothes?"

Helen realised that her mouth was actually open, and hastily closed it. She turned to the inspector. "Inspector—do I have to sit and listen to this?"

"No," he said, standing up. He walked over to her, standing close so that she had to hold her head at an uncomfortable angle to look at him. "No—you can talk, and we'll listen. I don't mind which. But I will tell you this. There seem to be only two people who were in a position to have killed Mrs. Mitchell. One of them is Wade, and the other is you."

"Me!" It had got too ludicrous for her even to be nervous any more.

"What did you think of your sister-in-law?" Sergeant Hill asked, as the inspector melted into the background once more, back to his desk.

"I didn't like her. I never have, and I'm not going to pretend that I did just because she's dead," Helen said. "I think you'll find that very few people liked her." Except Donald, presumably, she thought, then looked at the sergeant. Was that what all this was about? "Oh," she said. "I see. Someone's told you about her and Donald, is that it?"

"You know about that, then?"

"Yes." Helen stubbed out her cigarette in a shower of angry sparks. "Why? Were you going to spare my feelings?"

"If possible," the sergeant said. "But now that we've got it out of the way—I take it you weren't too happy about the situation?"

Helen lit another cigarette. "I couldn't have cared less, sergeant," she said. "My husband has had other affairs—in which I assume you have less interest—and I do assure you that the ladies are all still alive to tell the tale." She picked up the ashtray, and held it.

"But this was a little different? She had come into a great deal of money, hadn't she? Enough to tempt your husband away? Whereas, if she were to die . . ." she left the thought dangling in the air.

Donald! He thought he'd better tell them about the money. Now look where it had got her. Helen flicked ash nervously into the ashtray. "That's ridiculous," she said, because they seemed to expect her to say something. She looked across at the Inspector, but he had gone. "I don't care about the money," she said. "I didn't care about Julia, except that— except that I didn't know why he would prefer her. The others I could understand, but I didn't understand that."

A policewoman came in, with coffee, followed by Lloyd, who fussed round like a vicar at a tea-party.

"Sugar, Mrs. Mitchell? Milk?"

She didn't know what to make of him. One minute he would be like this, and the next he would be calmly suggesting that she killed Julia. On the whole, she preferred the aggressive Sergeant Hill, but that wasn't saying much.

He sat on the sergeant's desk. "Mrs. Mitchell," he said. She looked up at him. "We have no desire to charge someone for the sake of it. If you know anything about this business that you haven't told us, then please tell us now."

It was a trick. Frighten her into telling them something

that Chris hadn't told them. If she told them what he'd said, it would look as though he'd killed her. And he hadn't. He hadn't. It was a trap, she knew it was. But she couldn't see a way out of it. She shook her head slowly, her eyes tight shut. She had to tell them. Oh, Chris, she had to tell them. Tears oozed from beneath her eyelids, and she heard the door close. Opening her eyes quickly, she saw a blurred Sergeant Hill. They were alone.

"I saw his car at the roundabout," she said, haltingly. "And I didn't see him again until about six o'clock in the morning. He was drunk," she said. "He came to us for help."

Sergeant Hill nodded. "It isn't a betrayal," she said, gently. "He's told us what he can remember. But there are gaps."

Helen sniffed back the tears, and saw a warmth in the brown eyes that she hadn't seen before. "Will it help him?" she asked.

"If he's telling the truth, then you must tell the truth. It can't hurt him," she said, producing a small cellophane packet of paper hankies from her desk. Helen thought she probably had a tool for taking stones out of horse's hooves and spoke Chinese as well.

"He was drunk," Helen said again. "I couldn't make much sense of what he said."

"It's better not to try," she said. "Try just to remember the words. If that's possible."

Helen nodded. There weren't very many to remember. With what was left of her composure, she gave her account of Chris's visit, tearing the last of her privacy to shreds.

She had told her everything she could remember. When they had been left on their own, and he had begun to sober up, he'd gone quiet, and said nothing more about Julia. The clock behind the sergeant read twenty to ten, and she felt as though she had been here forever.

"Thank you," the sergeant said. "There's nothing more?"

"Nothing more about her," Helen said. "I don't have to tell you anything apart from that, do I?"

"No." She stood up.

"Do you believe me? Or do you still think I might have killed her?" Helen had no idea from her demeanour what she believed.

"We have to look at all the possibilities," she said.

"Oh—wait!" Helen Mitchell's face flushed. "He asked for her! He asked if she was there—he wanted to speak to her. He did!"

The sergeant sat down again, a dubious look in her eye.

"No—honestly. He did. He said 'Where is she? Is she here?' or something like that. He was too drunk to stand up—but he'd hardly be looking for her if he'd killed her, would he?"

The sergeant didn't seem as enthusiastic about it as she was.

"Is it true? Have you got Helen Mitchell here?" Chris jumped to his feet as Lloyd came in to the room, then wished he hadn't, and collapsed on to the bunk again. It didn't hurt unless he forgot. "Well?" he demanded. "Have you?"

Inspector Lloyd raised a disapproving eyebrow, and sat down beside him. "Who I choose to question is my business," he said.

"Why? Why her?"

"If she's here—why not? You've told me you went there on Sunday morning, and she's told me you didn't." He sighed. "It occurred to me that I'd given you an easy way out—I suggested that you'd been there. So now I'm asking her."

Chris subsided a little. Helen would at least confirm that. Every little helped. Unless, of course, she still thought she ought to keep quiet about it. "Has she confirmed it?" he asked.

"I don't know. If she does, she's in trouble and if she doesn't, you're in worse trouble. Wouldn't it be easier just to tell the truth?"

Chris massaged his temples, trying hard to keep his temper. "I am telling you the truth," he said. "Whoever killed

143

her is still running about and you won't look for him! You're so sure it's me—how do you know he isn't going to kill someone else?'' He lifted his eyes so that they were looking right into Lloyd's. ''I didn't kill her,'' he said, as though he were talking to a three year old. ''Do you understand?''

''I understand the words—but the evidence says different.'' Lloyd stood up. ''If she provoked you in some way—''

''She provoked me! She seemed to have a talent for doing that—and maybe somebody finally killed her for it, but it wasn't me!'' He lifted his leg up on to the bed so that Lloyd couldn't sit there again.

''Did she fall when you hit her?''

''I didn't hit her—no, she didn't fall. She stumbled.'' He lay back and closed his eyes.

''What's the difference?''

He knew the difference. ''She didn't fall over. She lost her balance, and recovered it.''

''Did she fall against the table? Cut her face?''

Chris opened his eyes to find Lloyd standing over him. ''No. As far as I know, she didn't hurt herself at all. But if there was a cut on her face, then there was. It didn't happen then.'' He swung his leg off the bed again, and reached for his crutch. ''Excuse me,'' he said, through his teeth. Jail would be peaceful compared with this.

''She hit her head on the table,'' Lloyd said. ''We know she did, so stop telling lies about that, at least.''

Chris stood by the wall, his fist hitting it disconsolately, impotently.

''All right. Who else did you have in your car recently?''

At least it was a different question. ''How recently?'' he asked, slightly disoriented by the new subject.

''Well, let's start with the same day. Saturday. We've found a set of fingerprints—they're not yours, and they're not hers. We just wondered whose they were?''

Chris frowned. Saturday? His brow cleared as he remembered. ''It was a girl,'' he said. ''She came to the garage looking for petrol, because she'd run out. I ran her back to her car. They must be hers.''

144

Lloyd was going into his amazed routine. "I'm lucky to find a petrol station that even employs people any more," he said. "And here you are, running stranded motorists back to their cars! I must remember that—is it a service you offer to everyone?"

Chris leant against the wall. "It was lunch time," he said. "I was closing up anyway. So I ran her back to her car. It's got nothing to do with this." He had forgotten her; she had been nice.

"Hasn't it? Fond of giving people lifts, are you? Pretty girls, at any rate?"

"I do favours for pretty girls that I might not do for you," Chris said. "I think you'll find that's quite normal."

Lloyd walked to the door. "If there's anything you know about Saturday night that you haven't told us," he said, "you'd better tell me now. I don't think you killed her—at least, not without help. But I'm going to have to charge you, because you're the only one I've got. If you're covering up for someone, believe me the favour won't be returned. You might get your reward in heaven, but here you'll just be sent to prison."

Chris pushed himself away from the wall, weary of the whole thing. "You know as much as I do," he said, and sank down on the bunk. If they thought he'd go to these lengths to cover up for someone, then they must believe the someone to be Helen. They thought she'd helped him—or that she had killed her. "And leave Helen Mitchell out of it," he said.

"Jealousy is unpredictable," Lloyd said. "Can't leave her out."

"You're wrong about that, you know. Donald wasn't seeing Julia. It's the girl that worked for her—used to work for her."

Lloyd looked faintly surprised. "No matter," he said, after a moment. "She *thought* it was Julia."

"I thought you were at work."

Donald had had more enthusiastic greetings in his time. "I came home to pick up some of Charles's papers," he said.

145

"Would you like to know where I've been?" She threw her handbag down on the sofa. "While you've been sorting out your nice rosy future?"

Donald was sure he wouldn't like to know, but he was going to be told, anyway.

"I've been to the police station—do you know I've never been in one before? When I do go, I'm on the wrong side of the law!"

"What made you go there?"

"What made me go there?" Helen tore open a new packet of cigarettes. "What made me go there was a six-foot-four policeman. Because you saw fit to bandy our business about!" She struck a match savagely, knocking its head off, and scrabbled in the box for another. "I believe I was taken in for questioning. They think I might have killed Julia, so that you could get her money!" She succeeded in lighting the cigarette at last. "Thank you, Donald. While you're choosing premises in Mayfair or whatever it is you're doing, I'm being accused of murder."

Donald sat down. They couldn't seriously think—but no, they obviously didn't, or she wouldn't be here.

"Failing that," she went on, "Chris killed her, but I helped him cover it up. I wasn't very good at it, was I?" She sat down, her hands shaking with anger, and blew her nose noisily.

Donald kept his distance, that seeming to be the safest thing to do. "They didn't seriously accuse you of all that, did they?"

"As good as." She relaxed a little. "Oh, it was just to scare me into telling them that Chris came here."

"And did you?"

"Yes. Relax, Donald. They've let me off with a smacked hand. And your name didn't even come up—not in that connection, anyway."

Donald frowned. "In what connection, then?"

"What do you think? Please stop pretending!"

Donald didn't know what to stop pretending about, and

146

that worried him. Before he could ask, Helen pushed past him, running out of the room and slamming the front door.

He looked out at the sky, picked up a coat, and followed her.

"Thank you, Mr. Muller," Lloyd said.

Mr. Muller was the driver of the brown Triumph Spitfire with the unreliable top. He'd seen the news, and he came as soon as he could get away from work to tell them that it was him. The rain had come on, and he'd stopped to try and get the top over, but it was stuck. So he had driven on with it down, and he had seen a lady in a car in the lay-by, who would, he supposed, be the one who had given his description to the police. It would have been about five past nine, because he was late for an appointment, and he'd looked at his watch when the bloody top stuck. He hadn't seen either the man or the woman, which was why he hadn't come forward before. He hoped he hadn't inconvenienced them.

"Someone helped him out," Lloyd said. "There were two people running about with her clothes."

"But she was in the car," Judy said. The phone rang, and she picked it up, saying yes and no when appropriate. "That was the lab," she said.

"And?"

"The phone has a number of prints on it, naturally. They'd need fingerprints from the normal users to sort them out. Is it worth it?"

Lloyd didn't know. "Perhaps—can they do anything without that?"

"They're checking the ones that are good enough, but some were obliterated. They say it had been partially cleaned with some sort of disinfectant. Probably one of those telephone wipes."

"That's all we needed. A hygiene freak for a boatman."

"That's the funny thing," Judy said, something obviously sparking off a memory. "We were in there on Sunday—do you remember? And that phone doesn't get cleaned. Not by any hygiene freak, anyway."

Clouds had rolled over the blue skies, and rain began to fall, at first in slow, large drops which fell into the pond and caused ripples to roll out, gently rocking the ducks. As it gathered strength, and the spots became small and determined, the odd groups of people who had gathered to look at where she was found began to disperse.

The ducks, fluffing out their feathers, wondered anew who had put out the rumour that they liked rain, and watched the people go. All except one, who sat on the bench in the rain, looking at them, but not seeing them. They swam up to be near her, and caught her attention. Looking round, she picked up a stray crust and threw it, but they could see that she had other things on her mind.

They all grabbed bits of bread.

CHAPTER ELEVEN

HELEN HAD SO FAR IGNORED DONALD'S ENTREAT-
ies to explain. She stared into the boating lake, its surface
spiked with rain, listening to the hiss, smelling the freshness.

"You had to bring her here," she said. "Because of some
silly game of yours, she's dead, and they think Chris killed
her."

"A silly game?" Donald sounded genuinely puzzled, but
she still wouldn't look at him. The grass, greener now that
the rain had come, stretched down to the road. And on the
opposite side, were the tall pine trees which had hidden Chris.
During the long summer she and Chris had walked in their
cathedral coolness, and they had hidden both of them. Now
everyone knew; they constituted nothing more than a woodland hideout, a place where a murderer evaded the police.

"I don't know what you mean," Donald said. "It isn't
sensible, sitting here in the rain—come home."

Sensible. What was sensible about any of it? She didn't
want to be here. Here, where it all started, where the summer
ended.

The rain grew heavier, and Donald took off his coat.
"Here," he said. "Put this on at least—you're getting
soaked."

She pushed the coat away. "Aren't you supposed to be at
work?" she asked.

"Yes. What's so terrible about that? Work goes on."

She shivered. "I wouldn't have believed you could be that cold-blooded," she said. "I know you don't believe in sentiment, but I thought I knew you better."

"Is this about Chris?" he asked. "I'm worried about Chris—you know I am! But there's nothing I can do about it—so I have to be practical. I've offered help—he knows he needn't worry about money. But I won't be staying in Stansfield, and the sooner I can sort it out and get out of your hair the better."

Helen could hardly believe he would take the game to these lengths. She stared at him. "Not Chris! Nobody would expect you to care about Chris, not now!"

"But I do."

"You do, don't you?" Helen stood up, and walked to the edge of the pool. Donald was by her side in seconds.

"Helen, I'm trying to understand." He wiped the rain from his face. "Can't we discuss this inside?"

"Discuss what?"

"Whatever it is we're discussing!" he shouted, turning away in exasperation. She watched as he squared his shoulders, and turned back. "I know what I'm like—you owe me nothing. I'm sorry if you want me to be insanely jealous about Chris, because I'm not. I'm glad you found him. I'm desperately sorry that he's in this mess—but I've done all I can!"

"This mess?" Helen shook her head, bewildered. "This mess? Is that how you see it? You've got money now, so it's an ill wind that blows no one good? I didn't like Julia, but surely she's entitled to more than that from you?"

"You're losing sleep over Julia?" he asked. "I don't see you in mourning!"

"I wasn't having an affair with her!" Helen cried, as the rain slackened off.

Donald opened his eyes wide. "And you think I was?" he asked, with total, unmistakable sincerity.

Helen walked slowly back to the wet bench, and sat down, regardless. Donald waited by the water, not looking at her. Her mind was full of all the little proofs of infidelity which had brought her to what had been a jumped-to conclusion. All the visits to London over the last twelve months "to see Charles about something," only to find out that Charles was abroad on business on at least two of these occasions. Without Julia, because Julia hated flying. A bitchy little hint from Julia herself, during the duty visit to them last Christmas, when she'd told Maria to remember that Mrs. Mitchell was here this time, and that the guest room should be aired. She had allowed the remark to hang in the air, for Helen to draw the inference that Donald on his own didn't need the guest room.

When Helen remembered the pay-off line, she didn't know how she could have missed what Julia was really trying to tell her. She had laughed as though realising what she had said, and added that Donald didn't mind roughing it in the servants' quarters. It would have infuriated Julia to know that her hint was lost on Helen, already firmly convinced that *she* was Donald's away fixture, as he had once himself disparagingly called his infidelities. That was when he was still promising to reform, a long time ago now. It was Maria, then. Attractive, quietly efficient, slightly withdrawn Maria who had taken his fancy, rather than the blonde and beautiful Julia. That must have peeved Julia, even if she had never given Donald a second glance.

"It's Maria, isn't it?" she said, almost apologetically.

"Well it certainly wasn't Julia," Donald said. "Give me credit for more taste than that."

It was hard to know what she felt about Maria—she had never taken much notice of her. She had gone to work for Charles in the hope, Helen had assumed, of catching him herself. But Julia had come along, and tricked poor, gullible bachelor Charles into marriage by pretending she was expecting his child. Charles, who had never wanted a wife, did want children, so that he could pass on all that he had worked for. But Julia wasn't pregnant, and had no intention of ever being, if she could help it. Charles had ended up with a wife and no children.

When Charles died, Maria was out of a job, and a home.

It had never occurred to Helen to wonder why Donald, of all people, cared, or why he had told her. But now she knew that it was all part of the game. And she had been too dense to work it out. Not Julia. Maria.

"Maria," she said aloud.

"I'm going home to change, and then I'm going back to work," Donald said. "Are you coming?"

She looked up at him, trying to come to terms with her new knowledge. He was looking holier-than-thou because he'd been wronged; slowly, she rose, and followed him home.

"Could someone have received a call at the boathouse?" Lloyd asked, having gone through every wild scenario he could to explain the wiping of the telephone. Even if someone had, it didn't get him anywhere, but it might stop him going round in circles.

"No," Judy said. "It's just an extension."

"Oh." Lloyd tapped his blotter with the top of his pen. "So she couldn't have called the police anyway?"

"Yes, she could." Judy smiled. "You get an outside line by dialing 9 first—she'd probably not know that, but I don't suppose she cared how it worked, so long as it got rid of Wade."

"Assuming it ever happened." Lloyd dropped his pen on to the blotter. "How come you know all that?"

"How do you think? Bob Sandwell, who knows everything. It used, he tells me, to be an ordinary phone, but whoever happened to be on duty would always find some friend in Australia to ring up. They couldn't leave it without a phone, in case of accidents in the boating lake. So they made it an extension when they got their new system in—now you can still dial out, but it's restricted to local calls."

"I'd better ring Mitchells—tell them we might need some fingerprints." He picked up the phone. "Why do I feel as if Wade's running this enquiry?"

Mitchells' Administration Manager agreed in principle to the fingerprints, but only if the men didn't mind.

"They might not have much choice," Lloyd said cheerfully. "But we might not need them, so don't spread any gloom and despondency."

"Do you think the phone was used when it happened?"

"It could have been, but there's nothing concrete."

"Because we can help you there," the voice said. "The phones are monitored now—we get a print-out with all the calls made."

Lloyd smiled. That was the first helpful thing anyone had said to him since this whole business started.

"When can I see it?" he asked.

"Let's see—Saturday. Picked up Monday. This is—oh, any time now. This afternoon, certainly."

Lloyd became slightly dispirited again. "It's possible that the phone was only picked up," he said. "It wouldn't show that, would it?"

"No. But if whoever it was started dialing at all, it'll show that. Time, date, the lot."

"Now, that could be just what we need. It would be at about nine o'clock, we think. You'll let me know when it's ready?"

"Certainly."

"Oh—by the way. Is it likely that someone would clean that phone at night? Cleaners, caretakers, someone like that?"

"Not very." He laughed. "We'll be only too pleased to get rid of the boating lake," he said. "As it stands, we man it, but it doesn't actually belong to us. We do the bare minimum—they sweep it out from time to time, but that's all. We did send out little packets of telephone cleaning pads when they all got their shiny new extensions, but in all that time only one extension's asked for a new supply." He laughed again. "And that wasn't the boating lake, so I doubt it."

"Thank you very much—I'll be round to collect your print-out as soon as you've got it."

Lloyd's subsequent enquiries revealed that no packet of telephone cleaning pads had been found.

"So," Judy said. "Either someone goes round with them

153

in their pocket, or they used the ones that were there and took them away. Why would you do that?'' She thought for a moment. ''If it had never been opened—you'd notice if one had been used. But you might not notice if it was gone altogether.''

Someone picked up the phone, used a pad to wipe the part that they'd held, and removed the packet. Lloyd picked up his pen to help him think. Wade? Why go to all that trouble if your prints were everywhere else? The same went for Julia, even if he could think of a reason for her cleaning her prints off anything.

He drummed his pen on his blotter, then let it roll away. ''If Wade's telling the truth,'' he said, ''he'd better pray that Julia starting dialling something.''

In the meantime, he had to tell Donald Mitchell that his sister-in-law's body would be released tomorrow, and he could go ahead with the funeral arrangements. They had traced Julia's father through the travel agent, and he was on his way home. He got a cool, unfriendly Helen Mitchell telling him that her husband was at work; he took the opportunity of telling her that they'd spoken to the driver of her open-topped car.

He got an earful from Mitchell himself, and put down the phone with some force when the call was terminated. They lied to him, and somehow it was his fault. He ought to do them both for attempting to pervert the course of justice. ''This bloody job!'' he said. ''I'm going to fetch my car.''

The phone rang again before he had even risen from the seat.

''Lloyd!'' he barked into it, unfairly.

''Inspector? Sergeant Hill was asking about the prints on the boatshed phone?''

''Yes, that's right. What have you got?''

''We've got a match—well, it might not be good enough to put into court—but it's good enough for me. A partial print on the phone matches the prints in Wade's car.''

''His prints?''

''No—not his. The other ones. The unidentified ones.''

154

Lloyd blinked. "But they're supposed to belong to some—right! Thank you. Mr. Wade's got a bit of explaining to do." He replaced the receiver. "So much for the lady who ran out of petrol," he said. "Someone helped him out, and he's not saying who."

"He could have known her before," Judy said. "She was scared—Diane MacPherson says so, Girvan says so. Even Wade says so, though I can't see how that helps him."

Lloyd tapped his blotter with his pen. "Perhaps we should let a doctor see him," he said. Wade could believe what he's telling us. Believe that he really did leave her alive and kicking. But the fact is that the minute Julia Mitchell saw him, she wanted to leave. And she didn't want him to give her a lift, and she looked scared before anything had happened."

Judy scratched her head. "Which do you want?" she asked. "Does he just go mad and kill someone and then not know he's done it, or did he know Julia and go after her, like she knew he would?"

"If someone helped him, and I'm sure someone did, then I think he just went bananas—that's why he says she looked scared. Because he doesn't know it was him she was scared of."

"Then how did Julia know to be scared of him in the first place?"

"Stop asking difficult questions. I don't know, but we don't have to prove any motive at all. What we want now is the owner of the fingerprints." He stopped talking, as yet another scenario presented itself. "Supposing Helen Mitchell did what you said in the first place? Hurried back from the station, went up to the café on foot—and found that Wade had just killed Julia. Her immediate reaction is to phone the police, but then she thinks better of it—wipes the phone, and they just run out to Wade's car. She ducks down so as no one sees her, then gets out and gets into her own car. That way she would see the kids leave, and Muller would see her. After she's had time to think, she goes back up there and tries to make it look like a sex crime."

Judy was giving him one of her looks.

"It's not impossible!"

"Why go back up there at all?"

"Because if she could make it look—" he stopped, because he didn't really know what he was going to say. "Maybe she didn't. She might have found him there with Julia exactly the way we found her. She got him out of there, then went home. But he turned up again at six in the morning."

The look was fading slightly. "It could have been like that," she conceded. "Rather than your first version—do you give your imagination full rein in front of anyone, or is it just me?"

Just you, he thought, but he didn't answer her.

"Her fingerprints," Judy said, "are on my ashtray."

Chris lay on his bunk, racking his brains, trying to think of anything that might make the police believe him. Had he been set up? But why? And anyway, he told himself sternly, that was nonsense. She was practically begging him to go away, and he could have, at any time. He needn't even have given her a lift in the first place. She hadn't asked him to. Had he walked into something, then? Someone else's murder? Could she have been meeting someone there, or what?

He sat up. That must be it, had to be it. She was meeting someone there—that's why she didn't want him along in the first place. And all that stuff about Helen—it was to make him angry, so that he would leave. What she didn't know was that whoever she was meeting intended killing her. Or ended up killing her, anyway.

He grabbed his crutch, and swung his way over to the door, using the crutch to hammer on it for attention.

"Hey! Can someone hear me? I want to see the inspector!"

He could hear footsteps, and the door was unlocked by a stout, balding policeman, who stood aside to let the inspector through.

"Your wish is my command, Mr. Wade," he said, smiling. "Have you decided to tell us at last?"

"No—no, I thought of something." In the presence of the inspector, waiting sceptically to hear what he'd thought, his solution seemed less and less probable.

"Go on, Mr. Wade," he said pleasantly, and sat on the bunk. "I'm listening."

Chris told him what he believed might have happened, as calmly as he could, and the inspector listened gravely.

"Now shall I tell you what we know?" he asked.

Chris looked suspiciously at him. "Something more?" he asked. "More than you knew before? I'm not going over the same ground again."

"Something new," the inspector assured him. "We know that whoever picked up the phone left their fingerprints in your car."

"I didn't touch the phone!"

The inspector was shaking his head. "No, I don't think you did."

Chris made an impatient noise. "Julia. I keep telling you. You know she was in my car."

"Not Julia. She didn't leave any fingerprints in the car."

Chris frowned. "Why not? She was in there."

The inspector shrugged. "She probably didn't touch anything. You opened the door for her to get in and out."

So he had. And she'd sat like a statue, with her bloody arms folded. He half laughed. "So I could have denied she was ever in the car?"

"Not really, Mr. Wade. There are other things. Her jacket, for instance—it was fringed. There were small strands of thread from it—that sort of thing."

Chris flopped down beside him. "What's the difference?" he said. "She *was* in the car."

"Quite."

"But no one else was."

"The prints say otherwise."

"I've told you about that!" Dear God, did he have to tell them everything eight times? "I gave a girl a lift!"

"And how do you account for this girl—whose name you don't even know—picking up the phone in the boathouse?"

157

"I can't." He hung his head, then lifted it again. "It doesn't make any sense," he said. "Unless she happened to use that phone earlier."

"It's a private phone—the public don't use it."

"Then I don't believe you!" Chris said. "Are you certain they're the same?"

"Yes." The inspector stood up. "I thought you might give up this nonsense."

"If they're the same," Chris said, "then they're Julia Mitchell's. What makes you so sure they're not?"

"Oh come on, Mr. Wade!" The inspector turned towards the door. "Even you must know about fingerprints!"

"Then are you sure it's Julia Mitchell you found?"

If his words had an effect, then he wasn't allowed to see it. The inspector left without turning back. The door banged shut, and Chris knew that he would go mad in prison.

It wasn't her. They had to check—they had to realise. She was running about somewhere—maybe she didn't know this was happening. Maybe she killed whoever that was that they found.

And maybe, he thought, as he looked round the cell, maybe he was going mad now. How many days could he stand, cooped up in a place like this? How many years would he be expected to survive?

Donald put the receiver back on the rest, and smiled grimly. Randall might not have said much, but at least he knew how Helen had been treated. Was it his imagination, or had he detected a subtle change in attitude? Was Randall ever-so-slightly deferential, now that circumstances had altered?

Funeral arrangements. He wondered if he ought to be doing something, but decided against it. Her father was on his way back, after all.

He picked up the particulars of a rather nice office suite, and settled down for a good read.

Judy got to her feet as Superintendent Randall came in, and was waved down regally.

"Is the inspector here?"

"Yes, sir—he should be back any minute." As she spoke, Lloyd came in.

"Good afternoon, sir," he said, smiling in the brittle way he did with people he didn't like.

"I believe you spoke to Mrs. Mitchell this morning," Randall said.

"That's right." Judy could hear the danger signals in Lloyd's voice. "She had been withholding information, as we suspected."

"But you don't suspect her of any serious involvement in this business, do you, Inspector?" Randall hadn't sat down, and neither had Lloyd.

"It's a possibility, sir."

Randall cleared his throat. "Look, I know there's been a bit of talk about her and Wade, but I don't think you should take gossip all that seriously."

Lloyd sat down. "We wouldn't get anything done at all if we didn't take gossip seriously," he said.

Randall looked for just a moment as though he might insist on due deference to his seniority, but if he was going to, he changed his mind. "True," he said. "But the Mitchells are acquaintances of mine," he added. "And I wouldn't like them to be dragged into this any more than necessary. In what way do you think Mrs. Mitchell could be involved? Just the fact that she didn't tell us Wade had been there?"

"Perhaps more than that," Lloyd said. "She could have helped him escape prosecution—or tried to," he amended.

Judy liked the 'acquaintances' bit. Just in case they were involved.

"Right. Can you prove it?"

"If she was involved, I should have proof shortly—there was a partial print found at the scene which may be Mrs. Mitchell's."

Lloyd explained how he had come by Mrs. Mitchell's prints, to the relief of the Superintendent.

"Let me know what develops," he said. With that, he was gone.

Lloyd made a face at his retreating back, and made no attempt to find him when something developed immediately. The phone rang, and Lloyd took the message, uttering terse and uninformative comments. He hung up, and looked at Judy with a mixture of disbelief and desperation.

"They're not Helen Mitchell's prints," he said. "I was convinced."

"Why are you looking like that?" Judy asked, though she couldn't have put a name to the look.

"Because Wade could be right."

"About what?"

"He asked me if I was sure it was Julia we found. Am I? Who identified her? Mitchell. Who comes into a fortune if she's dead? Mitchell."

"Oh, Lloyd." Judy shook her head. "No one would try that. Where's Julia then? And who did we find? It's nonsense—you know it is."

"I don't know it is. We made him think Julia was dead—I went to his house and *told* him she was dead. He sees visions of the good life, and then when he goes to identify her it isn't her. But he says it is." He picked up the phone. "We have to confirm the identification," he said, defensively. "It's a reasonable enough doubt."

But Judy remained unconvinced. It didn't seem reasonable to her. Could they really have been barking up the wrong tree all this time? "Her father's due back today," she said. "He could—"

"No," Lloyd said. "We've got the name of her dentist—I assume he doesn't figure in Charles Mitchell's financial provisions."

But surely, Judy thought, whoever it was would have been missed? You couldn't get away with—she thought hard. "The photograph," she said, at last thinking of some concrete rebuttal.

"You look at it," Lloyd said, "and tell me that you could swear that that was the girl we found."

Judy knew she couldn't. Old and blurred, her hair different, her face half turned. You couldn't tell.

"Guess who supplied the photograph?" Lloyd said, as he got through to the pathologist.

Some stopped and stared, pointed out to one another where she had been found, walked up to the barred door of the café, peered in the windows. There was nothing to see, but they did it all the same. They weren't there deliberately— they just happened to be passing, walking in the mid-day sunshine.

But mostly, people just went about their business. It had been news, it would be news again when the trial came up. For the moment it had been pushed to the backs of their minds along with Iran and Poland and the Vietnamese boat- people. They didn't stop and stare, these people with their own problems. They flashed by in cars, or walked past bus- ily, eyes fixed on the pavement ahead.

They didn't turn their heads. They didn't see the ducks, because they weren't looking. If ever they did look, they thought the ducks all looked the same. They didn't, of course.

But they did all answer the same description.

CHAPTER TWELVE

AGAIN AND AGAIN, CHRIS RETRACED IN HIS MIND
the steps he'd taken on Saturday. He was closing up for lunch
when the girl came; she was pretty, and tired, and hot—he
could see the perspiration on her blouse, as she waved at
him, to stop him from closing. He had sold her the petrol,
and chatted to her, the way you do. He had offered her a lift
back to her car, and then they had gone their separate ways.
He had no way of tracing her, of getting her to prove that she
was in his car, and that she hadn't touched anything in the
boathouse because she wasn't there. They were wrong about
that. He didn't care how reliable fingerprints were. They
were wrong about that. He'd driven on then, when he'd got
her back to her car—just an ordinary mini, like a million
other minis—on, into the countryside. A drive through the
villages that clustered round Stansfield, past the meadows
and fields that still looked like a Constable landscape; a drive
to clear his mind, to think about life in general and Helen in
particular.

He'd had no lunch, and spent the afternoon working, like
he always did. He was on his own in the garage on Saturdays,
a situation he kept meaning to remedy, and never had. Donald usually went to London at the weekend, and he would
normally close up and go straight to Helen's. But this Saturday Donald was home, and Chris was at a loose end. So,
he'd gone to see Elaine and Martin, arriving just in time to

be told that they had already eaten. They were expecting Donald and his sister-in-law round to discuss the boating lake, they said. His ears had pricked up at this—perhaps he could see Helen after all, and tell her what he'd been thinking on his countryside drive.

He'd been thinking that she should stop tearing herself apart, and tell Donald the truth. That there was no point in trying to play his game, and that you could only keep promises if there was a point to them in the first place. Once he'd made up his mind, he had been hardly able to wait for Donald's arrival. He was late—well, later than expected, and Chris had begun to think he might not come at all. But he had, complete with sister-in-law, and in the middle of a blazing row. They hadn't even come in properly, but had stood in the doorway to the sitting room, arguing, with poor Martin trying to sound jovial. Elaine and he had exchanged glances; they could only wait and see who won. Elaine had gone to the door, to try to rescue Martin, and then Chris had joined them.

It was then that she had said she was going, and Chris had realised that his chance might slip away. Donald might take her home, and by the time he could see Helen again, his resolve might have deserted him. And so, he had offered the lift.

She had said she was walking, and he had offered again, until she couldn't refuse. He remembered everything, like a slow motion film; she had tried to shake him off, several times, but he needed the excuse to see Helen. Donald might come home early if there was nothing to discuss; he had to have a reason for being there, for Helen's sake. He hadn't made himself objectionable, he was sure of that. He had simply said he'd help her look for her non-existent pen. Then the row had developed over Helen, and he had pushed her away as she came nearer to him, needling him. She had gone into the boathouse, and she had picked up the phone, screaming at him to go or she would call the police.

And he had given in, and left. He hadn't thought about

where he was going; he had just turned away from Helen's, and found himself at the garage.

And there, the memories of the accident had claimed him, and the horror of his inadequacy to deal with anything. He had found the bottle of scotch where he'd stashed it months ago, and he had started drinking. He must have fallen asleep; he heard the milk-float clanking its ghostly way up to the pumps, and it seemed very important that he put out the empty bottle. He had some sort of a conversation with the woman, and then he was on his own again, and he didn't want to be. And he was drunk, and Helen had made him promise that he wouldn't drink, and now he'd let her down. And he had left Julia there, in the bathhouse, almost frantic with fear.

So he had gone over on foot to Helen's, grimly determined to get there this time, to apologise to Julia, to tell Helen what he'd been thinking, to tell her he wouldn't let her down again.

He'd got there, eventually, and he may or may not have said any of the things he wanted to, because he had only vague memories of faces, and kindness, until his head had cleared and he was in the room on his own.

If only. If only he hadn't gone to see Elaine in the first place. If only he hadn't been so determined to see Helen. If only he had just dropped her off—if only he hadn't braked for the rabbit—maybe then he wouldn't have gotten drunk, and made everything so much worse.

He could see it now, darting out in front of him, and feel his foot going down on to the brake again—*again*, as if he hadn't killed Carrie that way. And Julia had gone shooting forward, but he had been going slowly, this time. Slowly enough for her to be able to catch the dashboard and stop herself getting hurt.

Julia, reaching out a hand to save herself. Catching the dashboard. "No harm done" she'd said, and she was holding the dashboard. *She was holding the dashboard.*

"She was holding the dashboard!" He leapt from the bed, and in one agonising leap was at the door. "I want to talk to someone!"

The same stout, balding policeman opened the door wearily.

"Keep your hair on," was his advice as he went in search of someone that Chris could speak to.

Chris waited impatiently, his hand on the wall to support him as he stood on his good foot, wriggling with impatience, like a child. The girl who had been with Lloyd during one of the interminable interviews came in.

"You wanted to see me?"

"Yes—look, she did touch the car. When I braked— remember? I told you. She touched it then, because she had to stop herself falling forward. She put out her hand and held on to the dashboard." He stopped, breathless, but there was no reaction from her.

"Don't you see?" he said. "Don't you understand? Those *are* Julia's fingerprints in the car. I said so to the inspector— it isn't Julia Mitchell's body!"

"But it is," she said gently.

"No! Check it, please. Check it again."

Her face was serious, almost sad. "We have," she said, quietly. "We found a dental card in her bag—everything that's found at the scene goes to forensic. And they're very thorough—they had already confirmed the identification. They told us about five minutes ago that there is no doubt whatsoever. It is Julia Mitchell's body."

Chris had to be helped to sit down. This time he didn't even hear the bang of the door as it closed behind her.

There was something about the way Judy came back into the office that made Lloyd look up from his desk. She was pale, and upset.

"What's wrong?" He went over to her. "What's the matter?"

"Nothing," she said briskly, visibly pulling herself together. "Nothing, except that I just pulled the lifeline away from a drowning man." She looked up at him. "He wanted to tell me that she did touch the car," she said. "That when they nearly had the accident, she caught hold of the dash-

165

board." There was a defiant tilt to her chin. "And I believe him."

Lloyd sat on her desk. "But they're not her prints—and you can't argue with that dental identification. We must have been right all along. He knew her from somewhere, or he had a brainstorm."

Judy had set her chin in its defiant attitude. "Then whose prints are they?" she asked.

"They probably are this girl's—the one he gave the lift to. The lab said they couldn't swear in court that the ones on the phone were the same."

"They said they might not be good enough for the court," Judy said. "But they were good enough for them—and you know that that means they're the same." She caught his hand, a thing she would never have done under normal circumstances. The efficient Sergeant Hill was letting her private life spill over into her working life. Lloyd wanted to smile, but he felt that he would get into trouble if he did.

"You were quite willing to believe that there were two people involved a few minutes ago," she said.

"But he won't say who it is!" Lloyd understood how she felt. Wade was convincing—he seemed to believe that he was telling the truth. But he couldn't be.

"Suppose he is telling the truth?" Judy persisted. "Lloyd, you've seen enough liars in your time! If you had no evidence but his word—what would you think?"

Lloyd blew out his cheeks. "I'd think he was telling the truth," he admitted.

"Then suppose he is."

Lloyd supposed. If he was telling the truth, then the body was not Julia Mitchell's. But the body *was* Julia Mitchell's, therefore he was not telling the truth. Oh no—that was pathetic fallacy or something. Faulty syllogism. All cows are quadrupeds, therefore all quadrupeds are cows.

"Wade has to be telling the truth," he said slowly. "Like a logic problem?"

"Yes," she said firmly, removing her hand.

Ah well, she'd gone back to being a policeman.

"Wade *is* telling the truth," he said. "And the body *is* Julia Mitchell's, therefore the person—" he broke off as WPC Alexander appeared at the door with a youngish man who waved an envelope at him.

"I'm from Mitchell Engineering," he said. "I've brought the print-out, because I thought you'd be interested—a call *was* made after hours." He handed the envelope to Lloyd. "I've done copies," he said, helpfully, but no one was listening to him. "I've marked the call with a red cross," he added.

"The call was made at four minutes to eight," Lloyd said, and knew that Judy's face mirrored his own in its complete lack of comprehension. He turned to the young man. "Thank you very much for bringing it," he said. "It's even more useful than I thought." He looked at it again. "Though I must confess I'm not sure how."

The young man smiled. "I can save you some time. The number rung was the Derbyshire Hotel's number. It just happens to be a number I know," he said shyly, rather as though it was a brothel.

"Lovely. Thanks very much—are you in a car, or can someone give you a lift back?"

"I've got the car, thanks." He smiled uncertainly, and left.

"Seven fifty-six," Lloyd said, uncomprehendingly. "But that's when Mitchell was there."

Judy nodded slowly. "She could have phoned someone without Mitchell knowing, I suppose."

Lloyd wondered. Mitchell had given him the impression that he and Julia were together all the time. But they were having a row, after all; he could have gone out to cool off or something.

"If she did make the phone-call," he said, "then she could have been meeting someone, like Wade said. And that's why she wanted to get away from the Shorts, why she didn't want a lift—let's go," he said, standing up. "At least we might be able to find out who got the call at the Derbyshire."

Judy was leafing through her notebook, reluctantly getting

to her feet. "Right," she said absently. "I just—" She shook her head. "I just think he's telling the truth," she said simply. "And if he is, then there must be a way that this lot makes sense."

"Maybe he's just not telling the whole truth," Lloyd suggested. "Like who was in the car with him?"

"Maybe."

The Derbyshire was just a short walk through the town centre.

"Four minutes to eight on Saturday night?" The manager, a small, fussy man summoned by a flustered receptionist, shook his head. "I'm afraid not." There was something triumphant about the statement, as though his inability to help were some sort of achievement. He pulled a hard-covered notebook towards him and flicked through the pages. "We log the calls out, of course. For the bills. But not in."

Lloyd groaned. "Were you busy on Saturday night? Full?"

"No, not particularly. About half-full, I'd say."

"How about people who were just staying over Saturday night?" he asked.

"One moment." The manager smiled professionally, and opened the register. "Four," he announced. "Four rooms, that is. Five people. One double, three singles."

"Could I have a note of their names and addresses?"

"Certainly."

"Did they all pay cash?" Judy asked, as the manager wrote out the names and addresses.

"I'll have to check that," he said, with just a hint of a sigh. He folded the piece of paper and handed it to Lloyd. "Excuse me."

"Any point in checking weekenders, do you think?" Lloyd asked Judy.

She shook her head. "I doubt it. If someone was involved in this, they'd leave as soon as possible. If we draw a blank we can come back to them, can't we?"

Lloyd nodded, and glanced at the list. The couple that the manager had mentioned, two men and one woman.

168

"Mr. and Mrs. Banks paid in cash," the manager said, returning suddenly and silently. "And Mrs. Williams."

"Neither of the men?"

"No," he said, by now clearly irritated. "Or I would have told you."

"Cheque—credit card?" Judy asked.

"Guests of local firms—we send accounts. I expect you want to know which firms, don't you?"

Lloyd smiled, and the manager went back into the office.

"You couldn't tell us what any of these people look like, could you?" Judy asked the receptionist.

"No, sorry. I was off sick on Saturday."

"Could you check the phone list again?" Judy asked. "See if any of these people made calls out?"

The girl, relieved to have something to do, took the list and busied herself with the log.

"Here you are." The manager had dropped all professional pretence at bonhomie in favour of a slightly surly approach. "Mitchell Engineering and Plasticraft."

Lloyd's eyebrows rose very slightly. "Thank you. Your receptionist is just checking something for us. By the way— would you be able to give a description of any of these people on the list?"

"No, it was my day off." He turned to the receptionist. "You would see them, Maureen—oh, no. You weren't here, were you? Who was?"

"Gina stayed on and did a double shift," she said.

"Don't tell me," he said to Lloyd, who had taken a breath. "You want her address."

"Please."

"No phone-calls," Maureen said, handing the list back to Lloyd. "Sorry."

"Just one more thing," Lloyd said, as he wrote down Gina's address and telephone number. "Have the rooms been booked out again?"

The manager consulted the register again. "Two of them have," he said. "The double and one of the singles—Mrs. Williams'. Why?"

"Could you keep the other two locked? We'll be sending round someone to take fingerprints."

The manager drew himself up to his full height, which fell short even of Lloyd's. "We do clean the rooms after they are vacated, Inspector."

"Well—you never know. Drawers, wardrobe shelves, that sort of thing."

They passed the lounge on their way out. "I wish it was opening time," Lloyd muttered, as they went out into the suddenly brilliant sunshine.

The sun slanted through the tall trees, but the pine wood was cool, as always. The sharp, clean smell that had almost gone during the rainless days was back, and Helen walked slowly, her feet snapping the tiny twigs that carpeted the ground.

Maria. Inside her head, the word was sung, as it was by the latter-day Romeo in West Side Story, and the tune wouldn't let her go. Maria, Maria, Maria.

All her married life, the rules had been simple. Donald told lies, and she pretended to believe them. Anything for a quiet life, for the right to call her soul her own. But she had broken the rules. She had *minded*, and she had refused to accept the lies. And now what? Now that she knew it wasn't Julia after all?

Surely he had been lying. Julia hadn't mentioned the boating lake—Helen couldn't see why it would matter to her what happened to it. Had she really only gone up there to count the salt-cellars? No. No, he was lying, he had to be. But now he was saying that he hadn't had an affair with Julia, and she knew just as surely that that was the truth.

She might have been the only person in the world, as she moved slowly through the pine wood. If she stopped walking, all she could hear was sporadic birdsong, all she could see was dusty sunlight through tall trees. All she could smell was pine.

But in her head, a voice mocked her, as she turned and headed for home. *Maria*, it sang. *Maria, Maria, Maria.*

* * *

Donald opened the freezer and looked at the rock-hard chops and steaks, the pizzas and sausage rolls, the labelled and dated pies and stews. Did you have to defrost them? Was that just chicken? The pizza declared itself to be at its very best if cooked from frozen in a preheated oven, and he expected he could manage that.

It hadn't surprised him when he had arrived home to an empty house, though he couldn't remember the last time it had happened. He didn't suppose that Helen would be cooking him too many more meals.

He'd checked the bedroom, to see if she had left him. But there were no clothes missing, no suitcases gone. He was glad. He should be the one to clear out. Helen liked it here, anyway. She liked the town and she liked the house, so obviously she must stay. He'd move out tonight if that made her feel better.

He had just consigned the pizza to the surely-preheated-enough-by-now oven when he heard the front door.

Helen looked pale, but she was calmer than she had been at lunch time, as though she had come to terms with something.

He smiled. "There'll be some pizza in about half an hour," he said. "If you want any."

But she just shook her head.

"We don't know she rang any of them!" Judy was annoyed at herself, not at Lloyd. She knew she was being negative, but everything about this business *was* negative. The finger-prints in Wade's car were not Julia Mitchell's, the telephone was not used after nine o'clock, there had been no sexual assault, though the body was naked.

"It's a chance," Lloyd said. "She's more likely to have rung one of them than anyone else—you said so yourself. And one thing we do know—Wade knows more than he's saying."

Judy didn't believe that. He wasn't the type—he'd have said something, let slip an unwary word, by now. He just wasn't clever enough, resilient enough, not to.

"He must," Lloyd said. "We know that there is another person involved now. Someone who was at the Derbyshire Hotel at four minutes to eight. There's a set of unidentified prints in Wade's car. Are you saying that's a coincidence?"

"No."

"Then what are you saying?"

"He says they're Julia's prints."

Lloyd sighed extravagantly, and slumped over his desk in mock exhaustion. "But we know they're not. Don't we?"

Judy nodded. So he was lying. But why? To protect this person? Something had gone on with all three of them up there, and he wasn't saying what. Her notes now contained the names and addresses of the Saturday night guests at the Derbyshire. The couple had been checked out, and were crossed off. The Plasticraft man was a buyer from Belgium, and he'd been crossed off. That left the Mitchell Engineering man and Mrs. Williams from Oxford.

"Why would he want to protect either of them?" she asked Lloyd.

"We won't know that until we know the whole story," he said. "But at least we've got the Mitchell connection—that might mean something."

"That's no connection at all." She moodily turned the pages of the notebook, not looking for anything in particular. "The Mitchells haven't had anything to do with Mitchell Engineering for years. He'll be another buyer, like the Belgian."

"Thank you. You are being a tower of strength."

Judy smiled her apologies, and turned the pages back again. Statements, opinions, names and addresses, facts. Facts were the only things you could depend on. No suppositions—no presumptions of guilt or innocence. Facts. Like a logic problem. And the facts could not be altered, only seen in a different light.

That light, at last, was dawning. Just a faint glimmer at the very edge of her mind, but it was there, if only she could find it.

* * *

The evening shadows lengthened as the sun dipped in the sky, and the woods grew dark. Around the boating lake, the gently rippling water reflected the sun's rays, casting pools of light on to the bark of the trees.

Across the road, the pine wood stood hushed and motionless in the still evening, silhouetted against the reddening sky. A light went on in one of the houses, as the tall trees blocked the setting sun.

The moth saw the light, and made her way towards it, fluttering up and down the glass in an impotent frenzy. There was a smaller window at the top; it was open. Perhaps she would stumble across it in her attempts to beat her way through the glass, and perhaps she wouldn't.

But it was there, if only she could find it.

CHAPTER THIRTEEN

"I'LL GO AND SEE MITCHELL," LLOYD SAID, LOOK-
ing again at the print-out. "See what he has to say about this
phone-call. Could you go and see Gina Whatsit—see if she
remembers either of the two we've still got to check—oh,
and before you do that, can you—" He could feel his words
hit the air and come back to him, like talking in an empty
room, and looked up from the print-out to find Judy neatly
ticking off notes in her pad.

"Are you listening to me?"

Evidently not. He walked over to her desk. "Come on—
we've got work to do. Leave the bloody notebook!" He
caught her arm, but she resisted in an abstracted way.

"It *is* a logic problem," she said, still not really speaking
to him, but to herself.

"Are you back on that?"

"No—this is different." She looked up, aware of him for
the first time in five minutes, he was sure. "That phone-call
was made at four minutes to eight. Right?"

Lloyd nodded.

"So either Julia herself or Donald Mitchell made it?"

"Yes."

"But neither of their fingerprints is on the phone."

"No." Lloyd pulled up the visitor's chair and straddled
it, his arms along the back. "Because it had been wiped."

"Who by?"

"By whom," Lloyd said. "Any of them, I suppose. Julia, Donald Mitchell—this person at the hotel, Wade." He shrugged.

"But Wade insists that Julia did touch the phone," she said. "So he'd hardly remove her prints." Judy was still turning the pages of the notebook.

Lloyd was puzzled, but interested. "He'd wipe it soon enough if his accomplice touched it, though," he said. "Whoever was in his car touched it, remember."

Judy nodded, the light of victory in her eye. "*You* remember," she said. "And while you're at it, remember that it was Wade who drew our attention to the phone in the first place."

So it was. "All right," Lloyd conceded. "Not Wade."

"Next question. *Why* did someone—not Wade—wipe the phone?"

"Please, miss, so that their fingerprints wouldn't be found," Lloyd said.

"What made them think anyone would be looking?"

"Dead bodies have that effect on people."

"*Julia's* dead body." She sat back. "Which rules out Julia, doesn't it?"

"And leaves Mitchell and the hotel-guest."

She smiled. "Mitchell and the hotel-guest—hang on to that, too." She pursed her lips in a determined effort to concentrate. "The partial print on the phone matches the ones in Wade's car. So it's reasonable to believe that those were the prints that someone was trying to get rid of. Mitchell had no need to get rid of his—he could have used that phone at any time without suspicion . . . the only reason for the phone being wiped is that it had prints on it that shouldn't be there."

Lloyd began to see the pieces more clearly. Not quite slotted together yet, but he had a feeling they were going to be.

"Bad acting," Judy said. "That's what Elaine Short said it was. Bad acting." She looked up. "Have you thought about that dentist's card?"

"Not constantly."

"What do you do with yours?"

"Dentist's reminders? Burn them," Lloyd admitted.

"I prop mine up somewhere," she said. "To remind me. And then I throw them away when I've been." She smiled, to prove how successful this method was. "I'm not saying she wouldn't keep hers in her bag—but wasn't it lucky? You find a naked body that could be anyone, and umpteen proofs of identity in her handbag, including the name of her dentist."

Lloyd thought about it. "Because it was important that she should be identified? However long it took to find her?"

"And think about what Girvan said about the time of death. The earlier the better—as early as the circumstances allow." She moved her pencil down the neat lines of writing. "Yes—here it is. We knew when she had last eaten, and he said that if you worked it out from that, it could give too early a time of death. He assumed fear—and we had reason to think he was right to—which slows the digestive processes down. So he ended up with a later time of death than he'd thought at first." She looked up, her face eager. "But supposing she wasn't afraid? Before people kept telling us she was, we thought she'd been taken by surprise, without a struggle, even. Which gave her no *time* to be afraid, and that brings you back to the early end of the range. Nearer eight o'clock? About five to eight?"

Lloyd sat up slowly. "Mitchell killed her? Then made the call to the hotel?" He got up, picking up the chair and putting it back against the wall.

"Mitchell. Who needed her to be identified. And who had to remove her clothes with care because someone else was going to wear them. Pretend to be Julia." She suddenly deflated, like a pricked balloon. "Except that Short already knew her," she said. "I should have known it was too good to be true."

"Did he?" Lloyd said, reaching for her phone, sitting on her desk.

"Yes. He even saw them on a dirty weekend at that hotel in London."

"Did he? Why? Why go to an hotel? Who'd go to a

176

crummy hotel when they'd got the run of what I gather is virtually a mansion?'' He asked for a number. ''I don't need notes,'' he said. ''I remember things.''

''Greenwood and Short,'' said a pert voice.

''Mr. Short, please.''

Martin Short came to the phone. ''Can I help you?''

''I think you can, Mr. Short. Lloyd, Stansfield CID.''

''Good afternoon, Inspector.'' Short was his usual affable self. ''How can I help you?''

''You mentioned something to me, Mr. Short. A chance meeting that you had with Mr. Mitchell in an hotel?''

There was a slightly embarrassed silence. ''Not a meeting, thank God,'' he said. ''I mean—he didn't see me.''

''When was this, Mr. Short?''

''Oh—about three weeks ago, I think. Just a second, my diary's here somewhere.''

It took a lot longer than a second, but Short came back to the phone eventually. ''Yes,'' he said triumphantly. ''Three weeks ago on Saturday.'' He flicked the page. ''It was the Sunday morning that I saw them, when I was checking out.''

''Thank you Mr. Short,'' Lloyd said. ''Two more things. One—how many times did you actually meet Mrs. Mitchell?''

''Three—if you count that time. Once, at her house in London, not long after her husband died, to discuss the various properties they wanted me to handle. The hotel—and then at our house on Saturday.''

''And two—could you let me have the name of the hotel that you were staying at, please?''

Short obliged, in a puzzled tone, but Lloyd merely thanked him, with no explanation.

''I think the much maligned Mr. Wade has been proved right again,'' Lloyd said, as he put down the phone.

''Right about what this time?''

''He says that it wasn't Julia Mitchell that Donald was seeing—it was her housekeeper. And the London hotel seems to bear him out—again. Why would Julia have to go to an hotel with him?''

Judy practically bundled him out of the door and into her car. Her haste was justified; Gina remembered Mrs. Williams well. She invited Lloyd and Judy into the flat that she shared with two other girls, both obviously pleased to have become involved in the murder enquiry, however vaguely.

"I checked her in," Gina said. "I remembered her because you don't often get women on their own. She was blonde—quite attractive."

"Did she go out at all?"

"Yes—she went out at about eight o'clock—just after I'd put a call through to her, so I thought she must have a date. But she was back just after nine, so I don't suppose it was."

"And, to coin a phrase," Lloyd said, "would you know her if you saw her again?"

"Oh, yes. I think so."

"We'll be in touch," Judy said. "You might be asked to pick her out of a line—do you think you'd be able to do that?"

Gina thought she would and it came as no surprise to them, when they got back to the station, to be told that Thames Valley couldn't trace a Mrs. Williams at the address given. Were Stansfield sure that the address was Oxford itself, or could it be one of the villages near Oxford?

They went into the office, and as the light flashed and flickered into reluctant life, Lloyd sat down with a sigh, feeling as though he had just got his mythical brother off a murder charge. He rang the number of the Mitchell house in London, and hung up when the phone was answered.

"I thought she'd move back in," he said. "Why not? Donald Mitchell owns the place now." He picked up the phone again, and rang for a car.

And so it was that just two hours later, they were standing on the doorstep of the Mitchell residence, which was indeed practically a mansion, inviting Maria Fraser to accompany them to the local police station. Maria was surprised to see them. She was attractive, as Gina and Diane had both said. Her hair was up, whereas Julia's had been down—fairer than Julia's, but who'd notice degrees of fairness? Make-up and clothes would turn her into an identical police description. Blonde, early thirties, denim skirt and jacket.

She complained, as they escorted her from the house, that she didn't know what was going on. Lloyd smiled when Judy assured her that she would pick it up as she went along.

He had never seen such a perfect match. She had caught the dashboard with the four fingers of her right hand, and she couldn't have done it better if she'd been trying to leave a set of fingerprints. Which, of course, she had been trying very hard not to do. She had done the only thing she could think of to stop herself touching anything. She had folded her arms.

No wonder, thought Lloyd, that she was none too keen to accept a lift from Wade. No wonder she looked scared, as he insisted on coming into the café with her. No wonder she was almost hysterical when he wouldn't leave.

She wasn't hysterical now. She sat between Judy and Lloyd on their way back to Stansfield, staring straight ahead, saying nothing, apparently calm.

"We'll be asking you to take part in an identification parade, of course," Lloyd said, conversationally.

"Of course," she said.

The car doors slammed, and Helen watched as the police drove off with Donald, under arrest. It hadn't really come as a shock—more, perhaps, as a relief, because the responsibility had been shifted from her shoulders. She had seen Donald's hand in it from the moment she realised that it was Maria with whom he'd been having an affair. It had all worked out too well.

Donald wasn't a lucky man—he made his own luck. Julia's death meant that he could have money, and Maria, and a clear conscience, because Helen would be provided for.

She had known him too long. He was worried about Chris—far too worried, because nothing really worried Donald that didn't affect him personally. Chris worried him, because Chris had blundered in where he wasn't wanted. And then there were the lies. The lies about Julia's obsession with the boating lake. Helen knew when he was lying; she always had. Walking on her own in the pine wood, trying to sort it out, she had realised that if the lies were not to cover up an affair, then they must be for some other reason. And the reason had to be the murder.

And now, she didn't have to choose. She stood in the sitting room where a moment ago the police had arrested Donald for murder, and she thanked God for saving Chris.

And yet she couldn't hate Donald, though she knew that he would have let Chris go to prison. She walked slowly out to the car, and prepared to enter a police station for the second time in her life.

Chris had thought he was going to be charged. He had prepared himself for that; he had decided to get a solicitor, to see what someone else could do, but in a way he had resigned himself to the fact that he had lost.

So that was what he had expected to hear, when the duty sergeant came to see him. Not that he was free to go. At first, the words didn't mean anything, and he felt like an actor who had been given the wrong cue. The sergeant went on to tell him that he might be required to give evidence, and still it didn't mean much. He was being shepherded out of the cell, up to the main desk. He was being thanked for his co-operation, he was being apologised to, he was being given back his money and his belt.

He asked if he could telephone his sister, and they said of course he could.

Donald saw Maria arrive, flanked by the inspector and his rather fetching sergeant, out of the corner of his eye, as he was taken into a small room and invited to stay there until the Inspector could see him. A burly young man stood in front of the door in case he should wish to leave.

After some minutes, both the inspector and his sergeant came, and he stood up to greet them.

"Sit down," Lloyd said.

"Don't worry, Inspector," said Donald. "We agreed— once Wade had got himself mixed up in this—that if you got

180

to Maria, the game, as they say, would be up. We can't even try to fight. You have a number of people who can identify her, I'm sure."

"Five or six at the last count," Lloyd said.

"It could have worked," Donald said, almost dreamily. "If young Mr. Wade hadn't been so keen to give her a lift home. None of these people would have been likely ever to see her again—and if they did, the passage of time would have made all the difference."

"You have been cautioned, Mr. Mitchell," the sergeant said.

"I have indeed," he said. "But it was a gamble, and we lost."

"Whose idea was it?" Lloyd asked.

Donald thought, and discovered that he really didn't know. He said as much to the inspector. "It was a joint enterprise," he said. "We both like the finer things in life, and neither of us counted Julia as one of these."

"You were very convincing," Lloyd said. "When I came to break the news."

"Oh, that." Donald shook his head, remembering the mind-numbing emptiness of that moment, when fact seemed to have overtaken the fiction that he had created. "That wasn't acting, Inspector. When I saw the state that Wade was in, and all the police arriving—I really thought that it was Maria you had found." He leant forward. "She is very important to me," he said. "More important than the money, I discovered."

"Julia Mitchell left your house at 7:30 P.M. on Saturday," the Inspector said. "Perhaps you'll take it from there?"

"Certainly," Donald said, and sighed. "I left with Julia, and told her I wanted her to see something at the boating lake. It was quite dark in the café—the trees block the light, you know—and besides, I had taken the precaution of removing the light bulb. It was really quite easy—much easier than I'd imagined." He looked from inspector to sergeant and back again. "I strangled her," he said.

The sergeant was looking back at him, her brown eyes widening just a little. "What with?" she asked.

"Tights," he said helpfully. "I've burned them, I'm afraid."

"And then you rang Miss Fraser at the hotel?"

"Yes." How did they know that? It wasn't supposed to end like this, but that's what gambling was all about. Tearing up your betting slip. "While she was on her way from the Derbyshire, I removed Julia's clothes—and Julia, I hasten to add."

The inspector opened his mouth, then seemed to change his mind.

Donald waited politely, then carried on when it seemed that the inspector was not after all going to speak.

"Maria and I went on to the Shorts—the idea was that she would leave almost immediately, in a huff. Start walking home, and disappear."

"While you were safely visiting the Shorts," the sergeant said.

"Quite. She would have gone back to the café, left Julia's handbag, changed back into her own clothes, and got rid of Julia's. Gone back to the Derbyshire, and left Stansfield on the Sunday morning."

Once again the inspector opened his mouth, a little hesitantly, but this time he proceeded with the question. "Why did you remove her underclothes?" he asked.

Donald looked and sounded like a professor answering a bright student. "I thought it looked better—you might have wondered, if they had been intact. Wondered why, I mean. So I took them off and hid them under a tree on the way back to the café. Maria was there by then, and we just went on our way."

"When did you plan all this?" the sergeant asked.

"The moment Julia gave Maria notice, I suppose," Donald answered. "Just after Charles died. It started as a sort of joke, really. Then Maria had to move into digs." The awful digs that she had hated, where the thought that Julia was

182

worth shoving under a bus had become less of a joke, and more of a discussion. "We realised that it might not be all that difficult. We saw snags, but not too many." He smiled. "And not the right ones, it would appear."

His audience did not respond, and he went on. "I arranged for Martin Short to meet Maria at Julia's—we had a key, of course. It was easy—we just had to wait until Julia went away for a while."

The sergeant was writing everything down, her pen making little swishing noises as she wrote.

"The meeting lasted quite a long time," he said. "But Maria was only there for a few moments. Just long enough for him to get a general impression of her. So that he would be a good witness when the time came." He smiled, a touch ruefully. "But when the time came, Wade happened," he said. "I imagine you'll be asking Maria about what happened then."

"We will," the inspector said. "But go on."

"He offered her a lift—she did her best to refuse, but he wouldn't take no for an answer. She couldn't go on refusing—the Shorts would have got too good a look at her. So she tried to get rid of him, but he stuck like a leech." He shook his head. "He even picked up that table and sat down for a nice chat. But you'll know that."

"Yes, we know that."

"In the end, she was frantic—she'd tried everything else so she grabbed the phone and threatened him with the police. It worked."

He sat back. "She tried to get rid of her fingerprints—was that the mistake?"

"One of them," the sergeant said.

"Well—she felt she couldn't just leave them. And she thought if she wiped the phone clean, you might wonder about that—so she tried to wipe the parts she'd held. We didn't think it would matter too much—her fingerprints shouldn't mean anything to you." If they did, he wasn't going to be told, he realised. "Anyway, she changed back into her own clothes which were in one of the boats, and walked back to the hotel. She rolled up Julia's clothes and threw them as far as she could into the wood.''

"Then *you* kindly provided us with a fuzzy photograph of Julia.''

"Yes—a bit too recognisable for my liking, but there weren't any others, except the wedding photographs, and we got rid of them. But there you are—that wasn't what let us down. Even after you'd got Wade, I thought we had a chance. He'd obviously seen nothing—he didn't know it wasn't Julia he was with. Maria even thought he'd done us a favour—taking the suspicion away from me, but I wasn't so sure. I'd have preferred it to have been an unknown assailant.''

"The best laid schemes,'' the inspector said, a trifle unoriginally, in Donald's opinion.

"As you say, Inspector. But I still don't understand why you were so reluctant to charge him.''

The inspector looked steadily at him. "You should have left the underwear,'' he said, shaking his head. "Two different people got rid of her clothes. That's what puzzled us, Mr. Mitchell.''

Oh, dear. Helen was always telling him about that. He always thought that if he added artistic little touches, he could get away with murder.

Judy pushed the typewriter away, and held her hands to the small of her back. "Done it,'' she said, but Lloyd had long since fallen asleep, his head resting on his hand. She looked at him for a moment, trying not to think of her marriage, or of what sort of future she might have, because it was too soon, and too difficult.

Last night hadn't been a beginning; they had known for years that it would happen one day. But it wasn't an ending—it wasn't an itch that they'd scratched and now it was gone. It was just another stage in their curious detached relationship.

Lloyd opened his eyes, as he realised that the typing had

stopped. "What did you want to do that tonight for, anyway?" he asked.

"It's tidier," she said. "And I don't have to come in to it in the morning."

"It is the morning," he grumbled. "Can we go now?"

"I've never been in court with you," she said, switching off the light as they left.

"No?"

"No. But I'll be there this time. I can't think why I didn't do it years ago."

Lloyd looked sleepily uninterested.

"You can't tell a court of law that your first name's David," she said, pushing open the door to the car park.

"Oh yes I can." Lloyd turned his collar up against the soft rain.

"But that's not your name." Judy got into the car, and pushed open the passenger door.

"It is now," Lloyd said, getting in beside her. "Officially, at least." He lifted the door, and closed it quietly. "I just kept the initial."

That ruled out Shirley or Marion, Judy thought. She grinned. "It's that bad? You actually changed it?"

"As soon as I was old enough. And I'm not going to tell you, so you might as well give up."

Judy began the process of starting the engine. "But other people know—people you grew up with. Went to school with—they know."

"Some," he said. "Which is how come everyone calls me Lloyd." The car coughed its way into a semblance of life. "Because they know," he continued, his voice flat, "that regardless of age, infirmity or sex, I will flatten them if they use it."

Judy put the car in gear and splashed it through the puddle that had formed at the entrance. "I'll find out," she promised him. "Somehow." She glanced across at him.

He closed his eyes. "No doubt," he murmured, sleepily. "But you're not exempt."

* * *

Stansfield was a carpet of orange lights in the darkness, as the owl flew silently over, on his way to a wood he knew where an owl could get a decent meal.

An old, dirty Ford Anglia made its way through the village, turning into the garages behind some flats. It disappeared as its lights went out. The owl flew on, towards the dark blot in the orange lights, towards his late-night snack.

He glided down, ghostly pale against the dark sky, and sat on the roof, motionless and ready. It was quiet tonight; the lake was dark and still. The gentle rain had barely dampened his feathers before it had stopped, and the night skies were clearing. It was pleasant, and cool, and not like the other night, when he'd perched here. When the storm was coming, and it had been so hot and heavy. That had been unpleasant. Yes, he thought, as movement caught his eye, and he swooped down upon his supper, that *had* been unpleasant.

In fact, that had been murder.

About the Author

Jill McGown is the author of seven mysteries. She lives in Corby, England.